Smog

JournalStone's DoubleDown Series, Book II

By

Lisa Morton

JournalStone
San Francisco

JOURNALSTONE
YOUR LINK TO ARTISTIC TALENT

JournalStone books may be ordered through booksellers or by contacting:

JournalStone
www.journalstone.com

www.journal-store.com

The views expressed in this work are solely those of the authors and do not necessarily reflect the views of the publisher, and the publisher hereby disclaims any responsibility for them.

ISBN: 978-1-940161-01-3   (sc)
ISBN: 978-1-940161-17-4   (hc – limited edition)
ISBN: 978-1-940161-02-0   (ebook)

Library of Congress Control Number: 2013941614

Printed in the United States of America
JournalStone rev. date: September 6, 2013

Cover Design: Denise Daniel
Cover Art: Alan M. Clark
Edited by: Norman Rubenstein

Dedication

To all of the 1960s denizens of 9th Avenue in Arcadia, who all share my reduced lung capacity thanks to the smog.

At least we only came out a little crazy.

Endorsements

"With *Smog*, Lisa Morton has created the perfect coming-of-age story. This is a tale of a magical time, with wonderful characters and a gripping plot that just won't let go. This is Morton at her very best, and you don't want to miss this one." – **John R. Little**, Author of THE MEMORY TREE, MIRANDA, and URSA MAJOR

"I'm sure SMOG by Lisa Morton is a true tale of terrifying horror. Or maybe she's just that fabulous of a writer. Evocative, provocative, and TOTALLY FREAKY. More!" - **Nancy Holder**, 5-time Bram Stoker Award winner and NYT bestselling author, DEAD IN THE WATER

Prologue

I was twelve years old in 1965. It was a year when the world felt like it was changing: Walter Cronkite reported on civil rights every night; we were sending troops to a country called Vietnam; men were walking in space, and the Rolling Stones were making rock and roll music sound *nasty*. Computers filled up entire buildings at NASA; the internet was decades away; our biggest war was cold, and telephones were still things that were wired into walls.

I had the perfect family, living the American dream: Mom and Dad, two kids, a three-bedroom house in a little suburb of Los Angeles called San Diablo, located out at the eastern end of the San Gabriel Valley. Fifteen years ago, the whole area had been orange groves; now it was a middle-class neighborhood that centered on families supported by the local aerospace industry. The houses all had nice front lawns and pools in the backyards; there were cocktail parties for the parents and birthday parties for the kids, and the most successful fathers bought brand-new color console television sets that weighed as much as refrigerators.

It was all perfect...until something went wrong with the smog. It was so thick that on most days we couldn't see the foothills at the end of our street. A lot of us kids were no good at running because of the smog—it would make your lungs burn and seize up after half a lap.

Breathing problems, however, were the least of what the smog was doing to us.

Of course we didn't know that when it all started to fall apart...

Chapter 1

"The moon just blew up!" That was what CJ said when he came running into the house that day in June 1965. It was almost eight in the evening.

CJ was my older brother. His real name was Charles Robert Donohue, Jr., but he hated Charles, Charlie, Chuck, Bob, and Junior; CJ was the only iteration he didn't hate from a young age. Of course I shouldn't say anything—I go by Joey even though my birth name is Michaela Jo Donohue, but come on, *Michaela*? Back when they'd both been young and growing up in West Virginia, my parents had known someone who'd named her little girl Michaela, and for some inexplicable reason they'd been smitten by the name. I, sadly, have never been able to say the same. Fortunately I was a tomboy from birth, so "Joey" suited me just fine.

CJ was pretty decent, as older brothers go. He was four years older than me, but he'd never bullied me or been otherwise mean. When we were both little, he'd let me tag along on his expeditions. True, he'd once put a Jerusalem cricket—possibly the biggest, ugliest, worst-smelling insect found in all of Southern California—in my bed and laughed like crazy when I'd screamed. But he'd apologized afterward, and I frankly sort of thought Jerusalem crickets were cool—they reminded me of the big plastic bug in my Cootie game. I'd made him take the cricket back out to the dirt trail that ran between our backyard and the fenced-in, concrete-lined runoff channel we all called "the wash."

I also liked CJ because he was always popular at school. He'd been elected class president at San Diablo High when he was still a freshman. I liked his friends and girlfriends, and (much to our scientist father's horror) he wanted to go into politics someday. He planned on majoring in political science at college, and he was smart enough that his counselors at school figured he'd land a scholarship with no problem. CJ's popularity was good for me, too; because people liked him, they automatically liked me. Well, at least a few did—I've never been as good at the handshaking and glad-handing thing. I had Debbie Curtis, who'd been my best friend since before either of us could even talk, and sometimes we hung out with Matthew Visser, who lived halfway down our block and was weird enough to be both intriguing and kind of scary...but otherwise I didn't have a lot of friends. Not like CJ did, anyway.

1965 didn't start off seeming so different. I was in my last year of elementary school and was looking forward to starting junior high in the fall; CJ was a high school sophomore. By June, all of the kids were out of school, with three glorious months of summer freedom before us. CJ was usually off with his friends, Mom had all of her social activities, and as for Dad...well, we never saw Dad anyway, so I'd have the house all to myself for most of the summer.

That summer had started with two events I most especially remember: On June 3rd, Ed White became the first American astronaut to step outside the safety of his Gemini capsule and into outer space, and we watched the event on our brand-new color Magnavox television while my mother glowed with pride (and a few martinis) and told us, "That fellow wouldn't be out there if it weren't for your father." What exactly Dad had to do with the space walk, I don't think Mom had the vaguest idea. We only knew that he worked in the aerospace industry, often spending weeks out at Edwards Air Force Base in the middle of the Mojave desert.

The second big deal was the Rolling Stones. "(I Can't Get No) Satisfaction" was released in that same month, and suddenly the rock and roll music that all our parents had decided they could live with because it wasn't going away got *dirty*. Every night, as the sun went down on another hot Southern California summer day, all the teenagers would saunter out to plop down on their front lawns with transistor radios tuned to station KHJ, waiting for the next play of "Satisfaction." You could walk along the street, the sky still barely light overhead, and hear that guitar riff echoing out of dozens of tinny little handheld radios. I wasn't quite old enough yet to hang out with the rest of them, but I liked the song (which I somehow guessed had something to do with— *gasp!* —sex), and I liked being able to hear it all up and down my street.

What I didn't know then was how those two things—space stuff and teenagers—were about to intersect. Nobody knew, not even my father...and he was responsible for it.

This particular June evening, Mom and Dad and I were inside; it was one of those rare nights when Dad was not only home but was home early. Mom was washing up after dinner; Dad was scanning the newspaper, and I was rereading a *Fantastic Four* comic (featuring the Sub-Mariner, whom my pre-adolescent self had developed kind of a crush on). CJ had been outside with all the other teens, but he suddenly came rushing in through the front door, breathless.

"The moon just blew up!"

We all kind of stopped and looked up at him, waiting for the punch line or something; but instead he kept going. "I swear, something's going on—there's a huge part of the sky where the moon should be that's all lit up and full of smoke and stuff!"

"That's ridiculous," Dad said, putting his paper down.

"Dad, you gotta come and see!"

I didn't wait for Dad—I got up, went to the sliding glass doors that led out to the backyard, and ran out.

Sure enough, a big section of the sky overhead was glowing, way brighter than the surrounding areas shading toward dusk, and there seemed to be a sort of roiling rim around the glow. A few seconds later Dad joined me, and I heard him whisper, "I'll be goddamned."

That was weird for two reasons: first of all, nothing ever surprised my Dad; and secondly, he never used curse words.

"What is it, Dad? Is it the moon? Did the Russians blow up the moon?" We were all obsessed with the Russians, who we were convinced were determined to nuke every last American.

"No, of course not. The moon's fine. It's a rocket test. One of ours."

We'd seen rocket tests before, of course, living in the cradle of America's aerospace industry...but they were usually just tiny white trails in the sky, not huge white splotches like this.

I looked from the sky to my dad and asked, "Did you work on it?"

My dad stared at the sky for a few more seconds before turning away. I thought I heard him murmur, "This shouldn't have happened."

He left to go back to work right away. He didn't even answer when Mom asked him if he wanted to take a thermos of coffee.

The next day, the smog had taken on a strange, yellow tone that I'd never seen before. It blotted out the sun and erased any blue. It made all of our eyes burn.

It was just the beginning.

Chapter 2

That was the summer I was crazy for movies and spy stuff. I loved anything to do with detectives or secret agents—my favorite television show was *The Man From U.N.C.L.E.*, and I wanted to be the female James Bond. I'd spend my afternoons alone in the house trawling all four of our local stations for mystery movies, although I'd settle for monster movies or science fiction if the spies were all out in the cold.

Three days after we all thought the moon had blown up, CJ came running into the house, excited again about something. It was three in the afternoon, and *Journey to the Center of the Earth* with James Mason and Arlene Dahl was starting on Channel Nine's *Million Dollar Movie*. I was just settling in with a bag of Fritos and a glass of chocolate milk when the back door banged open, and CJ hurtled in like something was nipping at his heels.

I tried to ignore him, intent on our heroes' discussion about an Icelandic volcano, but when he picked up the phone and said, "I need the police," Professor Lindenbrook suddenly became less interesting.

"I want to report a dead body," he said. I got up and turned down the volume.

I realized that CJ was as white as a proverbial sheet, and his hands were shaking; this was no joke.

"There's a dead girl in the wash behind my house," he said.

That was all I needed to hear—a dead body, right behind my house? This was like living inside a detective show! I had to see for myself. I set down the Fritos and headed out to the backyard. In the far fence was a gate that opened onto the dirt road beside the wash. I knew that CJ sometimes walked home that way from his girlfriend Vicki's, because he could sneak out the back if her parents came home unexpectedly.

CJ looked up from the phone, saw me in the backyard, and deduced my intention. "Wait a second," he said into the phone, then put his hand over the mouthpiece and yelled at me, "Joey, DON'T!"

"But I wanna s—"

"Trust me, you do *not* want to see this."

"Yes, I do."

I walked away, knowing he wasn't about to hang up on the police to come after me.

I opened the gate and walked out onto the dirt road. It was a narrow, gray-brown strip bordered by the wooden fences of houses on one side and a chain-link fence keeping intruders (meaning kids) out of the wash on the other. The wash was pretty uninteresting most of the time—at least 350 days a year it was a bone-dry concrete ravine with nothing in it.

But today, I looked down and saw something a short distance ahead. I walked forward, my heart thumping in excitement and nervousness. Finally I reached the point where I stood directly opposite it and looked down from maybe thirty feet away at:

It was a dead girl, but not like any dead girl I'd ever seen in a movie or television show. I thought of the murdered woman from *Goldfinger*—the one Bond finds on the bed painted gold—and how elegant she'd looked in death.

The dead girl in the wash wasn't elegant, though. She was sprawled in a strange position, one leg bent awkwardly under her, one arm akimbo, hair partially obscuring her face. Her clothes—a simple, button-down blouse and a skirt—had been torn away from her, as had her undergarments. One breast was exposed, and her panties were down around her knees. Somehow I knew that hadn't happened in a fall.

And there was blood—a lot of it, mostly around and beneath her. She was lying in a pool of her own blood, although it took me a few seconds to realize that was what I was seeing—it looked darker than I thought it would. It almost looked more black than red, especially under the odd light cast by the smog.

I tried to imagine how she'd gotten down there and could only figure that someone had thrown her body over the fence and into the wash to dispose of it.

After they'd raped her and murdered her.

No, this certainly wasn't like a movie. My stomach was churning, my heart still pounding…yet I couldn't stop staring.

I didn't look away until I heard CJ shouting at me. "Joey!" He came running down the dirt road until he reached me. "The police are on the way. You probably shouldn't be here when they come."

"How could somebody do that? They killed her and then…threw her away…"

CJ put a hand on my shoulder and tried to steer me back to our gate. "You shouldn't have seen this. Let's get you home."

I allowed him to direct me, but my eyes wouldn't turn away from the dead girl. "Do you know her?"

CJ shook his head. "I can't really tell with her face covered by her hair."

"Me either."

As we reached the house, we heard the first approaching siren. "Stay here, Joey, okay? Promise me you'll stay here."

"I promise."

I felt cold in the middle of the afternoon heat, and I had no desire for any more dramatic events. The dead girl was the worst thing I'd ever seen.

That would change soon enough.

Chapter 3

Mom arrived a few minutes after the cops. They were out back with CJ when she came rushing into the house, panicked over the police cars with flashing lights parked outside her home.

"Joey! Oh my God, baby, is everything all right? Where's CJ?"

She hugged me so hard I had to pull away to talk. "He's okay, Mom. He's just out back talking to the police."

"What happened?"

"CJ found a dead girl in the wash."

Mom pulled away to look at me in shock. "What…?"

"Yeah. It's pretty weird."

"Did you see it, too?"

I nodded, and Mom pulled me into her again, and it felt good, warm, safe.

"Oh, my poor baby."

"It was awful, Mom. There was blood and she was…she was…" I broke off. If I said anything else I was going to cry, and I didn't want to cry while there were cops around my house.

Mom got me settled down on the couch and then went out back in search of CJ. I knew she was worried about him, but I also knew he was going to catch a little hell for letting me see the body.

I almost told Mom not to go back there, not because it hadn't been CJ's fault that I'd seen the corpse—I was always happy to let CJ take a little heat—but because when Mom had hugged me I could smell alcohol under her Doublemint gum.

My mom wasn't exactly an alcoholic, but she did like her afternoon cocktails with "the ladies." A lot of the moms on my street were members of the San Diablo Women's Club, which met every weekday afternoon, either at their own clubhouse (yes, they had their own clubhouse), or—if it was Thursday—at the bowling alley. Their meetings were supposedly in part about fundraising—feeding starving children in Africa or some such thing—but what they were *really* about was a bunch of frustrated, bored, middle-aged housewives getting together to get sloshed.

If you're under 40, you may not realize how different things were back then. The women's movement was still nascent, and most women were expected to just have kids and stay at home keeping things clean and organized for their hardworking husbands. A few cocktails everyday didn't mean someone had a drinking problem; it meant they were *social*. My mother was good at being social.

Which is not to say she was bad at being anything else. I actually thought she was a pretty great mom, and so did my friends. She talked out problems with us, she was fair when she had to discipline us, she was proud of my little accomplishments (like when I'd won an essay competition for fifth graders), and at 40 she was still attractive, while some of the other moms were getting a haggard, used-up look (due in part to cigarette smoking, which was still chic).

My dad was the mystery—literally. I knew he had something to do with rockets, but I wasn't really sure what. He wasn't a cruel or uncaring man, but he was always kind of distant, as if his mind was already up there with the stars.

Sometimes after he'd been gone at Edwards for a few weeks, he'd come home and bring me amazing stuff—little models of space capsules or signed astronaut photos. I wish I still had all that; it'd probably be worth a small fortune now. I think I gave some of it away to friends at school, but I have no idea what happened to the rest.

The week of the dead girl, Dad wasn't at Edwards, but wherever he was working (some aerospace company—there were a lot around here), he was pulling nonstop late nights. I heard Mom on the phone to him, telling him what had happened, but halfheartedly ending the conversation with, "No, we're okay. I can handle it." She looked a little lost when she hung up.

An hour later, she and CJ and I sat down together to watch the local news. There was a mention of the dead girl found in the wash. Her name was Mary Ann Wilson, and she was a year ahead of CJ at San Diablo High. Mom asked CJ if he knew her; he said he thought maybe he'd seen her around, but he didn't know her beyond that.

I just thought about how Mary Ann Wilson had been somebody's daughter and probably somebody's sister and somebody's best friend, and she certainly didn't deserve what had happened to her. Nobody did.

The news report ended by noting that police were "still investigating," which I knew meant they had no suspects. Whoever had done this to Mary Ann was still loose.

There was a killer in our neighborhood.

Chapter 4

The next day, Debbie's mom, Marge, took us to a matinee: *The Sound of Music.* I think she was trying to cheer me up, but I hated musicals, and I don't think Debbie was nuts about them, either. Marge left the theater singing, though, so I guess she was happy.

I was still thinking about the murder victim—Mary Ann Wilson. I couldn't get the image of her torn, exposed body out of my mind, no matter how much Julie Andrews sang and pranced about. Marge offered to take us out for ice cream after the movie, but I lied and said I wasn't feeling well, when I really just couldn't stand the thought of being around Marge while she kept humming those songs. I liked Marge okay most of the time—she was a small, chipper woman who smoked too many cigarettes and had bad teeth as a result—but today I just wasn't up to her perpetual cheerfulness. I wanted to be in my bed with a pile of comic books.

When I got home, I made myself a glass of chocolate milk and was on my way to my room when I heard strange sounds coming from behind CJ's closed door. I paused to listen, and instantly knew this was something I wasn't supposed to hear: He had his girlfriend Vicki in there, and they were both kind of moaning and gasping. I could also hear an odd, rhythmic creaking sound, which it took me a minute to place as bedsprings.

A jolt of disbelief shot through me as I put it all together: CJ was having sex. With Vicki. In his room. Right now.

I had only the faintest idea of what was involved with sex. For one thing, I was a little behind the other girls my age—Debbie, for example, had already been having periods for a year (I knew this because one day at school a sanitary napkin had fallen out of her book bag), and she even had actual *breasts*. Her breasts were big enough that the boys at school paid a lot of attention to her, and I sort of envied that. Even though Mom had bought me a training bra, I was still as flat as a pancake and didn't wear it most days.

Mom had explained a few basics to me, so I knew that men had parts women didn't have, and that sex started with kissing and ended with babies, but I was still kind of uncertain about what happened in between. That's why it took me a few seconds to place the sounds coming from behind CJ's door.

I stood in the hallway, the glass of chocolate milk forgotten in my hand, and listened, feeling both guilty and excited. I was confused, too, though—it sounded like they were hurting each other. The sounds continued for maybe another minute—their cries sharper, the creaking faster—and then it died away.

Next they giggled, and then I heard CJ saying something about going out to the kitchen. That was my cue to make like a banana and split. I started to run for my room, but then I had a better idea, and headed out to the kitchen, where I plopped myself down at the dining table just before CJ walked in.

He was shirtless and his hair stuck up in a zillion different directions, but at least he'd pulled some pants on. He literally froze for a second when he saw me. "Oh…I didn't know you were here," he said, as he tried to pretend to casually amble over to the refrigerator. "I thought you'd be out all day with Debbie and her mom."

"No, I got home about twenty minutes ago."

He tensed at that but got two cans of Coke out of the fridge. He elbowed the refrigerator door shut, then leaned against it, eyeing me warily. "So, you…uh…"

I started to moan, doing what I thought was a pretty good impression of Vicki.

It must have been a *great* impression, because CJ gritted his teeth in anger and then caught himself. "You gonna tell Mom?"

I took my time answering, letting him squirm a little. "I might…but I could maybe be persuaded not to…"

"What do you want?"

"A dog." It was true; I'd been bugging Mom for months now for a dog. She always said that dogs were a lot of trouble and she didn't think I was responsible enough to help take care of it and so on. I knew that if I could get CJ to promise to help with it, though, she might reconsider.

CJ rolled that around in his head for a minute. "A dog, huh? Would I have to help take care of it?"

"Maybe a little at first. Just long enough to convince Mom to let us keep it."

"And you won't say anything about…?" He jerked his head towards his room.

I ran a finger twice across my chest. "Cross my heart. Of course Mom might figure it out on her own when Vicki shows up with a baby that looks like you."

"Not gonna happen, twerp." He reached into his pants pocket and pulled out a little square foil packet. It looked like candy to me. Was there a candy that could keep a girl from getting pregnant?

CJ turned then and went back to his room. I heard his door close behind him and some low giggling. But I wasn't really listening anymore—I was already trying to think about what kind of dog I wanted.

It turned out to be a good thing we never did get that dog. There's no way it would have survived that summer.

Chapter 5

A day later, Debbie told me that Matt Visser had been asking her if it was true that I'd seen the dead girl.

Every neighborhood has an obligatory weird kid, and Matthew Visser was ours. Nobody knew what had happened to his mother; we only knew that Matt lived with his father, and spent a lot of time alone because his dad was always working.

Matt was a smart kid—he'd tested insanely high on his IQ test—but he had a mean streak. I wondered sometime if his dad beat on him, and Matt carried it on down the line and abused other kids. He had this toy that heated up and could cook little rubber monsters, and he loved to try to lure the unwary into touching the burning-hot surface. He'd fry ants with a magnifying glass on summer days or put dead cockroaches on a girl's chair at school. He'd spent more time in the principal's office than anyone else in school. You'd think Debbie and I would have avoided him like the plague.

But we didn't. Maybe it was because he lived two houses down from me, and we'd all grown up together, or maybe Debbie and I secretly felt sorry for him, because he didn't have a mother or siblings, and we seemed to be his only friends.

Debbie thought it would be fun to go tell Matt about my encounter with a corpse, so we went to see him.

We knocked on his front door, and after a few seconds he answered. "Oh, hi, you guys," he said, regardless of our gender. "Hey, you gotta come see this – I've got something really great to show you."

Matt had dried blood on his white T-shirt.

"Are you okay?" I asked him.

"Yeah...why?"

"Is that blood on your shirt?"

He stopped in the kitchen doorway and glanced down. "Oh, yeah, I guess it is. S'okay, though—it's not mine. Now c'mere."

We followed him into the kitchen. I noticed the smell—foul and musky—before I saw what was on the kitchen table.

Matt had laid out some kind of animal there. It was dead (from the smell I was guessing it'd been dead for a while), but it was so badly mangled it was at first hard to make out what it'd been. Then I saw the big, fluffy tail, and I guessed we were looking at a squirrel that'd been hit by a car.

"God, Matt, that's *gross*," Debbie said, grimacing.

Debbie was putting it mildly: this was weird even for Matt. "Where'd you get it?" I asked.

"Found it this morning in the gutter over on Camino Real." He stuck a finger in the thing's split side, and something bluish-grey poked through the matted fur. "You think that's the liver?"

"I don't think you should touch it," I said.

He looked at me with surprise. "I thought you liked dead bodies."

"No, I don't, and why would you think that?"

"You found Mary Ann Wilson, didn't you?"

"No, my brother did."

I didn't like the way Matt's eyes were glistening—he reminded me of a rabid dog. "But you saw her, didn't you?"

"Well...yeah...but there's a big difference between seeing something and liking it."

Matt shrugged. "If you say so. Hey, want some ice cream?"

The idea of eating anything near that rotting little carcass made me nauseous. Something was really wrong with Matt, and I was starting to think leaving sounded like a great idea.

Debbie wasn't going to let him off the hook so easily, though. "What's your dad going to say when he comes home and finds this mess all over the kitchen table?"

Matt stuck a finger in the squirrel again. "Maybe Dad's not coming home."

I started for the front door. "C'mon, Debbie..."

She followed me but couldn't resist a final jab. "Yeah, let's leave Doctor Frankenstein here to creating his perfect bride." But Matt wasn't listening; he was too busy poking through the squirrel's innards with that grimy finger.

When we got outside, I stood on the sidewalk, trying to figure out what bothered me. It took me a second, but I finally got it: Matt's dad's car was parked in the driveway.

I knew then we'd never see Mr. Visser again. At least not alive.

Chapter 6

They arrested Matt three days later. That was when a man named Bruce Morrison, who worked with Matt's dad, stopped by the house to see if everything was okay and noticed the smell. At first he thought it was just the dead animal in the kitchen, but then he realized it was too strong, and he followed it into the back bedroom, where he found Mr. Visser's corpse, pulverized by a blast from a shotgun. We all knew that gun — Matt had bragged about how his dad had once taken him duck hunting and let him fire the gun a few times. When the police questioned Matt, he confessed immediately. Later on they said he showed no remorse.

I believed it.

Two dead bodies in a week would have been weird enough in our quiet little suburb, but there was other stuff going on, too.

CJ had been bringing Vicki home every afternoon, but the same day that Matt Visser was arrested, CJ brought Vicki *and* his best friend Larry home. Vicki didn't look too happy when they all went into CJ's room together and closed the door; when she came out 15 minutes later, she was still half-undressed and crying.

"Are you okay?" I asked her. I wasn't in the habit of chatting with my brother's girlfriend, but she looked like she could use a friend today.

When she finally pushed her hair aside and turned to look at me, I saw a bruise on her cheek. She was still buttoning up her blouse, pausing to brush tears away.

"Your brother's a real jerk," she said, before running out of our house.

I heard CJ and Larry laughing in my brother's room.

It was the first time in my life I'd ever been afraid of my brother.

It wouldn't be the last.

Chapter 7

The next day, Debbie was bored and asked me if I wanted to walk down to the five-and-dime. Her older sister had gotten a job there, and Debbie said we could get free candy. Besides, I was hoping they might have some new comic books in.

Debbie's sister, Sandy, was 19, but she wasn't smart enough for college, so she'd gotten this job as a clerk at the dime store. We all knew that she was really just killing time, though, until she could snag some hapless guy for a husband and start popping out brats. She was no beauty queen, but she knew how to flirt, so we all kind of figured it wouldn't take long.

Unfortunately the trip was a bust; she couldn't get us free candy, and this month's comics hadn't arrived yet. Plus, Sandy was making goo-goo eyes at some young guy in a suit, and she hissed at us to "Beat it!"

I'd never especially liked Sandy.

On the way out of the dime store, Debbie paused by the racks of candy bars, took a quick glance around, and then pocketed one. I was shocked and immediately nervous; I'd never seen Debbie commit any sort of criminal act before. I was just certain we'd be apprehended at any second, squads of hidden security men swooping down on us with drawn guns and handcuffs.

"What are you DOING?" I whispered to her.

"Shut up. Let's go."

She rushed us out of the store, then began to giggle once we were out on the sidewalk.

"I can't believe you just stole from your sister's store," I said.

"Oh, lighten up. It's just a candy bar. Besides, it's not my 'sister's store'. She's only a stupid clerk."

"I think you should take it back."

She pulled the candy bar out of the pocket she'd stuffed it into, tore the wrapping off one end, bit off a third of it, and then, as she chewed, said, "You're right—I'm taking it back."

I had to laugh, both at her trying to talk around a mouthful of chocolate and at how brazen she was, to stand in front of the store she'd just stolen from and eat her pilfered goods right there. She ate the rest of the candy bar and then said, "I think you should take the next one."

"I'm not a thief."

"Oh, well pardon me, Miss High-and-Mighty. Maybe you'll feel differently if you ever come down out of that ivory tower and join the rest of the world. C'mon, *everybody* steals."

I didn't want to believe that, but after what I'd seen happening to my friends recently, it was starting to sound more plausible.

"I'm not high-and-mighty. You make me sound like Julie Andrews."

We were passing an auto parts store, and Debbie patted me on the shoulder and pointed inside. "Oh yeah? Well, then, here's your chance to prove it."

Steve Noonan was inside, talking on the phone behind the front counter. Even from out here I could see he wore a striped button-down shirt with a sewn-on patch above the front pocket that read "Steve".

Steve was a year ahead of Debbie and me in school, which meant he'd started junior high last fall while Debbie and I were finishing elementary school...but he'd already been huge a year ago. Now, at 13, he was nearly six feet tall, with broad shoulders, thick blonde hair, and the beginnings of a downy growth above his upper lip. Debbie had once caught me staring a little too long at Steve, and she knew I thought he was cute.

"What's he doing in there?" I asked Debbie. "He's not old enough to work..."

"His dad owns this store. I hear the old man's trying to train Steve to take over the business."

As we watched, Steve hung up the phone and scribbled notes on a pad of paper. Debbie slapped my arm. "C'mon," she said, as she opened the door and went in, leaving me standing on the sidewalk in the grip of anxiety.

"Debbie!"

But she'd already reached the front counter. "Hi, Steve," I heard her say.

My heart hammering, I walked up to join her.

Steve was peering over the counter at her. "Hi...uh...Debbie, right?" Then he saw me, and the recognition was genuine—and more than flattering. "Hey, Joey, long time no see."

"Yeah. Hi, Steve." I felt heat in my cheeks, and knew I was blushing.

"So how's good ol' Jackson?" Andrew Jackson was the name of our elementary school.

"It's fine. How's Morrison?" That was the junior high, where Steve was now ensconced.

"Dumb. Boring. You know." He shook his head, and I liked the way it made his hair kind of bounce around. I felt myself blushing again.

I knew Debbie saw it, because she snorted laughter and then said to Steve, "So, Steve—how are the junior high girls?"

He grinned. "Well, you'll find out in September, won't you?" Then he stared at me, with blue eyes the color of the sky before the smog set in, and I almost turned and ran.

Debbie motioned at the door. "I guess we will. We'll see you later then—"

Steve cut her off, still looking right at me. "Hey, are you busy the rest of the day?"

"Ummm...no..." I said, hating the way my voice came out, kind of wispy and barely audible.

"Wanna do something? We could just watch television, or play a game..."

"Don't you have to work?"

"To hell with this." He tore off the striped work shirt, revealing a plain white T-shirt underneath, then vaulted over the front counter while shouting, "I'm done!"

He'd taken three steps forward when a huge, bear-like man staggered out of the back. Even from across the room, I could tell that this was Steve's dad (he looked like a bigger, bald, wrinkled version of Steve) and that he was drunk...not like the way my mom got drunk when she "lunched with the ladies," but drunk as in he was weaving, and his words were slurred, and his eyes were red. "Where the hell you think you're goin'?"

Steve didn't turn to face him, but just kept heading for the exit. "Anywhere away from here."

"Get your ass back here NOW!" the old man bellowed from behind the counter, but Steve was already through the door and out on the sidewalk. He didn't slow down as he hit the street, and Debbie and I had to almost run to keep up with him.

"Old drunken asshole," Steve muttered, and I blanched; I'd only heard "asshole" used once before, when my dad had gotten mad once at a guy who'd stolen a parking space from him. My mom had chewed my dad out for "using that word in front of the children," and I'd never heard it since.

Until today.

Steve continued to rail against his father for another block, and then he stopped and looked around. "Hey, can we go to your house?" he asked me.

"Uhhh…sure."

Debbie shot me a look that was half-impressed and half-jealous, but my insides were already churning…we were just going to watch TV, right? What if Mom came early and saw me with a boy she didn't know? Would she be mad? And what about CJ? He'd been so weird lately there was no telling what he might do.

But I led the way to my house. When we reached it, Debbie told me to call her later, and she crossed the street to her own place, making a kissy-face at me once before turning.

"Hey, this is okay, right?" Steve asked. I thought it was cool that he was being so polite.

"Sure, of course. My mom won't mind."

"Is she here?"

"No. She's off at her Women's Club meeting."

I opened the front door and led the way to the living room. Steve followed behind me, looking around, making a low whistling sound. "Wow, this is really nice. My house is a dump." His eyes really lit up, though, when he saw the Magnavox. "Is that color?"

"Yep. Hey, you want something to drink? A Coke?"

"That sounds really good."

I got two cans of Coke, handed him one, turned on the television, and sat on the couch. An afternoon variety show came on, Herman's Hermits were the musical guests. "These guys aren't bad," Steve said, in-between gulps of soda, "but my band's better."

"You've got a band?" I know I sounded like some starry-eyed fan, but I really *did* think that was neat.

"Yeah. I play guitar. We're pretty good. We're writing our own stuff, and I think we'll get our first gig soon. I'm gonna become famous, and then we'll see what Dad says about how I have to work in that stupid store. I'm sure not gonna throw my life away behind the counter of some two-bit car parts shop. Hell, no."

Steve talked for a while longer about his band and the other guys he played with and how long he'd practiced guitar, and I was actually starting to get bored. I wondered where CJ was. I hoped Herman's Hermits came back to do another song. I hoped Steve would either change the subject or leave soon.

Finally, he said, "So, what about you? What do you want to do when you graduate?"

"I'm not sure yet. Everybody says I've still got plenty of time to decide."

Steve nodded, finished his Coke, and then said, "You got a boyfriend?"

The heat was back in my face. "No..."

"Why not? You're pretty. I used to notice you when we were both at good ol' Jackson."

"Really?"

"Yeah. Of course." He set his empty can aside and said, "Hey, want to play a game?"

"Sure." I thought maybe he meant Monopoly, or Parcheesi. Instead, he said, "Okay. First you gotta close your eyes, though."

I giggled. "Are we going to play tag?"

He laughed, too, then said, "No, smarty-pants, we're not going to play tag. Now close your eyes."

I did, still giggling.

"Okay, now raise your right hand."

When I did, he took it in his hand. Part of me melted right down into the couch. I couldn't wait to tell Debbie that he'd held my hand. "Now, don't open your eyes," he reminded me.

"I won't."

He pulled my hand down. "You have to guess what this is." He pushed my hand down onto what felt like the rough denim cloth of his pants but with a strange lump just underneath—it was big and hard but kind of quivered as I touched it. My first thought was that it was something alive, something he had in his pocket.

"A frog?"

He laughed, but the sound was deep and husky. "Guess again," he said. He put his hand on top of mine and pressed it hard against the bulge.

Suddenly I knew what it was. I jerked my hand away and leapt up from the couch, remembering the torn and violated body of Mary Ann Wilson. Was Steve her killer? Her...*rapist*?

I stood there shaking and terrified. Below me, Steve was rolling his eyes and motioning for me to calm down, but I couldn't take my eyes off his crotch, the way it was swollen out. I was ashamed by my own stupidity, my gullibility. I was an idiot. And now he might rape me because of it.

"Are you..." I couldn't get out the words. "Are you going to..."

"Look, calm down." He got to his feet and towered over me, and I stood there like a dumb animal, waiting for the predator to pounce, knowing I could neither outrace him nor fight him off.

Instead, he started for the front door. "Sorry, I thought you were...well, older, I guess."

He left.

I didn't watch him go. I stood rooted to where I was until I heard the front door slam. Then the tears came. I ran to my room, closed the door, and threw myself onto my bed. I cried harder than I'd ever cried in my life. I'd never felt so stupid, so betrayed.

An hour later the phone rang. By then the sobbing had subsided to the occasional sniffle, so I got up to answer the call. It was Debbie, of course, asking what happened.

"Nothing happened." There was no way I could be honest, even to my best friend.

"*Nothing?*"

"We watched TV for a while. Then he left."

"Are you okay? You sound kind of stuffy or something."

"Yeah, I think I'm allergic to something around here. That's mainly why he left."

"Oh." I knew she was disappointed, but it was better than admitting the truth: that he'd tricked me into touching his thing.

"I've gotta go, Debbie," I said and then hung up on her.

I cried some more, until I heard Mom come home. I forced myself to stop; I knew if Mom asked me what was wrong, I might just start blubbering in front of her. Instead I didn't come out until my eyes had dried and the red had faded. Fortunately she looked like she'd had more than one martini and didn't notice anything.

"Did you do anything fun today?" she asked, as she fixed dinner.

At least I wasn't lying when I said, "No."

Chapter 8

I didn't sleep much that night. Instead, I thought about what had happened with Steve. By dawn I'd decided I had to start acting more like Pussy Galore; she'd dropped James Bond himself in a judo throw. Maybe I could talk Mom into letting me take judo lessons, but in the meantime I needed something else.

I came out for breakfast and put on a good show of bored kid on a summer day. Then, I waited until everyone else had left, and I went into Mom and Dad's bedroom. I remembered that Dad had an old pocketknife with one broken blade that he'd left on top of his dresser; I didn't know why he hadn't thrown it away, but it was just the right size for me and the main knife blade was still fine. I had no idea if I could actually use it if I had to, but I felt better with it in my pocket.

Debbie's mom was taking her clothes shopping today, and I had no idea where CJ was. I was getting bored, but I was too afraid to leave the house and go anywhere. I really wished Mom had stayed home. We could have watched television together, or played games, or even cleaned the house.

God, I was twelve years old and I wanted my mommy.

That was pretty pathetic, but I didn't care. I *did* want my mom. She'd always been there for me; she'd taken my side in fights with Debbie or CJ; she'd encouraged me when I became interested in new subjects, and she'd even read my schoolbooks so she could help me with homework. But she was at her club today, socializing with the ladies.

I decided to go see her. The clubhouse was only a few miles away, and on my bike it probably wouldn't take me more than half an hour to get there. Plus, I could pedal faster than anyone could run, so I'd be safe.

I got my bike out of the garage and headed off. The smog was terrible today, and after just a few blocks I was gasping for breath. I stopped at a park to use the drinking fountain and stared up at the sky; it was an ugly, hot-mustard color and obscured anything more than a couple of miles away. I heard a shriek and jumped, then relaxed when I saw it was just a couple of six-year-olds messing around on the park's swing set. They were laughing and having a good time, and I envied them.

Don't grow up, kids — the world gets weird.

I rode the rest of the way to the clubhouse on Duarte, parked my bike outside, and went in. The building was a little, round stand-alone structure surrounded by a parking lot and across the street from a bank and a liquor store. The main door opened into a small alcove that was occasionally used as a box office, when they had special events. Just beyond it was the central room, a wide space with a few tables scattered around and a little stage up front.

I was about to go in when I heard a woman crying.

I didn't like to hear adults crying, because I knew that meant something was *really* wrong. I almost turned around and left, but then I heard my mother's voice consoling the crying woman, and curiosity got the best of me. I stayed out of sight in the alcove, listening.

"...can't believe it, it's like she's not even the same person. She was always such a *good* little girl."

A number of voices murmured condolences. Another woman, not Mom, said, "I know. I'm having the same problem with Darren. He's been a straight-A student his whole life, and now all he wants to do is smoke cigarettes out in the garage."

A little thrill of recognition went through me. Was she talking about Darren Johnson? He was legendary at my elementary school, the smartest kid they'd ever seen, etc., etc. I'd heard he was doing equally well in junior high, and was on track to be valedictorian one day. He fit the part, too: a tall, gangly kid with a crewcut, glasses, and shirts buttoned all the way up.

It was almost impossible to picture Darren Johnson lounging around with a cigarette dangling from his lips.

The crying woman continued to blubber. "I just don't understand what happened...it's like she's not even the same person."

A calmer voice replied, "She's sixteen now, Doris; she's not supposed to be the same person."

"But not like this...my girl could never have been *mean*..."

That drew a chorus of "I've got the same thing" and "I know" and "These kids today" responses.

I fell back against the wall, realizing: it wasn't just CJ, or Steve Noonan, or Matt Visser, or Debbie stealing candy bars; it was every teenager in town, apparently.

I left without letting Mom know I was there. It seemed like her friends needed her more than I did right now. After all, I'd finished my crying yesterday.

And I was determined that I would never cry again.

Chapter 9

Dad came home that night at a decent hour; he even beat Mom, who was surprisingly late.

"Where's your mother?" he asked, as he set down his briefcase and took off his jacket.

"I think she's still at her club."

Dad just sort of nodded, then went to the kitchen to mix himself a drink. He and Mom loved manhattans, which I'd once tried a sip of and nearly gagged. I waited until he was settled in his recliner with his drink and his paper before I said, "Dad, there's something weird going on..."

He eyed me over the top of his glasses. "Such as...?"

"The older kids. The teenagers. They're all kind of..." I searched for the right word, then remembered what the crying woman had said at the club today. "...of *mean.*"

Dad looked at me for a minute, then said, "But *you're* an older kid—a teenager."

"No, Dad—I'm twelve."

"Oh."

I loved my dad dearly, but it's a fact that he was often clueless where his own children were concerned. He got our ages mixed up and forgot stuff like our birthdays or friends' names. It's not that he didn't care; it's just that he always seemed to be somewhere else in his head.

"But...CJ..." I said, prompting him.

"What about CJ?"

"He's..." I tried to figure out how to say what I suspected without making Dad think I was nuts. "He's been bringing Vicki home in the afternoons. Almost every day. They go in his room and shut the door, but I can still hear them."

"Hear them doing what...?"

I felt my face go hot. "You *know*, dad."

He looked at me for a long time, then finally said, "I'll talk to CJ about that."

"That's good, but...have you heard about the dead kids?"

Irritated, he ruffled his paper and lowered it. "Joey, what is this really about?"

"Everything's been kind of weird since that..." I thought back, and suddenly I knew. "...since the moon blew up!"

"The moon did not blow up."

"Well, you know...since that rocket exploded."

Dad visibly tensed, and for a second I wondered if whatever was making the teens crazy was in the adults now, too. "Don't be ridiculous, Joey."

"But it's true—"

Dad cut me off, leaning forward, and now his tone was kind of desperate, pleading. "Promise me right now you'll never say that to anyone else."

"Why?"

"Just *promise me*."

The look on his face was nothing I'd ever seen before, and I gulped before I said, "Okay, I promise."

He seemed relieved by that, and his face relaxed. "And I'll make you a promise: everything's going to be fine. Okay?"

"Okay."

My dad wasn't a real physical guy, so I didn't get up and hug him, but I did sit on the couch and watch the evening news with him. I was glad he was there when CJ came home. At least my brother didn't have Vicki or Larry with him.

Maybe whatever had happened was starting to fade. Maybe my dad really had had something to do with it but had fixed it since. Maybe the Russians had tried something, but my dad had saved us all.

I went to bed believing that one.

I should have realized it was just the quiet before the storm.

Chapter 10

The next day was the summer's first real scorcher; I spent most of the day lying around inside the house with cold drinks and comic books. By the time evening came, I was bored and wanted to go outside to cool off.

As always, the older kids were all out on their front lawns with their transistor radios, rock and roll echoing through the suburban dusk. The sky was fading from smog-yellow to smog-red.

I didn't see CJ at first, but it was impossible not to notice Debbie's older sister Sandy. She was dancing to the music on her lawn, wearing the smallest skirt I'd ever seen and a low-cut blouse, and she had a ring of boys at her feet, all looking up at her with rapt expressions.

One of them was CJ.

What was he doing? Didn't he care that Vicki might see him? Wouldn't she get mad?

Well, if she wasn't mad already, she certainly would be at what came next: CJ disengaged himself from the circle of boys, stood up, and started dancing with Sandy. He put his hands on her hips and looked right down her shirt and pressed himself up against her. She grinned at him and put her hands on his shoulders. The other boys started hooting and urging them on.

They got closer and closer. By the time the song ended they were practically *doing it* right through their clothes.

Sandy leaned in and kissed CJ. He kissed her back. She pulled away, took his hand, and led him into the house. The other guys were screaming by now.

And then I saw Vicki. She was on our side of the street, two houses up, watching, frozen, her expression one of shock.

I promptly marched into my house and called Debbie. She picked up on the third ring.

"Did you see who just went into your house with your sister?"

I heard her snicker, and then she said, "Oh, I know. You should hear them right now—they're going at it like two animals." Debbie laughed again.

I didn't get it. Why was Debbie laughing? Didn't she think it was completely awful that my brother was having sex right now with her sister? "Isn't your mom…doing anything?"

"She's not here. She and Dad went out to dinner with friends tonight. Wait a minute…" I heard her put the phone down, then there were voices—Debbie and another female voice—then Debbie came back on the line, sounding breathless. "Oh my God, you're not going to believe this: Vicki just came in, and she is *furious*." Debbie giggled again and said, "I gotta go."

The last thing I heard was shouting. Then the line went dead.

I hung up, walked into my room, and closed the door. My brother was crazy. My best friend's sister was crazy. Heck, my best friend was crazy.

I didn't come out until morning.

Chapter 11

"Are you up?"

It was Debbie on the phone. I yawned and glanced at the kitchen clock—almost nine. I guess I'd finally fallen asleep near sunrise. "Sort of," I answered.

"Get dressed. There's something you have got to see. I'll be right over."

I would've preferred a slower morning, with a nice, long shower behind a locked door, but I knew there was no denying Debbie when she sounded that determined.

I'd just barely thrown on a shirt and some shorts when she rang the front doorbell, then burst in through the front door. There was no sign of anyone else; I guess Dad had already left for work, Mom was at the club, and CJ was...well, who knew where.

"So what's this big thing I've got to see?"

Debbie waved me to the back door. "C'mon!"

She slid it open and stepped into our backyard. *Why is she going into my yard?*

Then I realized she was really heading for the gate and the dirt road beyond. "Why are we going back there?"

"Trust me, this is amazing!"

I trudged through the yard, past the hibiscus bushes, and over the dichondra lawn, until I joined her. "Let me guess: somebody threw up in the wash. Wow."

"Oh, it's a lot better than that."

I followed her out onto the dirt path and saw immediately that, maybe fifty yards away, there was something big draped over the chain-link fence that lined the sides of the wash. I paused, feeling my gut clench. Debbie danced ahead of me, vibrating with excitement. "Hurry *up*!"

It was a body. I could tell even from a distance. It was somehow draped over the top of the fence, whether deliberately or as the result of an attempt to dump it into the wash, who knew. I slogged along after Debbie, who'd already reached it and stood beneath it, pointing up and giggling. "C'mon, you haven't even seen the best part yet."

I wanted to turn around then, go home, and lock the doors, call Mom, call the police, call anyone...but I kept walking forward, like a prisoner marching to the gas chamber, every step heavier than the rest.

Blood had formed a huge, spread-out pool beneath the body, but Debbie didn't seem to care; she stood in the middle of it, and I saw that lots of other bloody footprints already led away from the pool. The head hung upside down, facing away from me. I skirted as much of the blood as possible—I was just wearing cheap rubber sandals and the idea of it getting on my toes made me nauseous—until I'd moved around to where I could see the face.

It was hard to make out the features, since the head was upside down and covered in blood from the slit throat and multiple stab wounds, but the long, blonde hair gave it away.

Vicki.

The strength ebbed from my legs, and I plopped down in the dirt, staring up at her. Her open eyes were filmed with blood; what was left of her clothes were tattered and stained red; her arms and legs hung down on opposite sides of the fence.

"Isn't this the *coolest*?" Debbie grinned at me as if it was Christmas morning and Santa had just brought her a puppy.

"Did you find her?" I said. My voice sounded strange, too high-pitched and soft.

Debbie laughed. "No, silly."

"Then how...?"

"Are you kidding? *Everybody* knows she's here!"

Debbie turned and stuck a finger into a stab wound on Vicki's stomach, and my mind flashed back to Debbie telling Matt it was gross when he did the same thing to a squirrel.

I forced myself to my feet and turned to leave.

"Where are you going?" I heard Debbie ask.

I didn't answer. Before I knew it, I was running. I didn't look back. Behind me, Debbie shouted, "Don't be such a chicken!"

I ran through my yard, slammed the glass door shut, and turned the lock. Debbie would have to take the long way around to get home again, but I didn't care. I didn't ever want to see her again.

I was about to run to the front door to lock that when CJ stepped into the hallway in front of me. "Where you been, little sis?"

He was covered in blood. It was on his hands, his shirt front, his face, even in his hair. I knew whose blood it was.

"None of your business." I ran past him.

"Hey!" he shouted, but I ignored him, fled into my room, shut the door, and moved my desk chair under the knob. I was still getting it just right when the door shuddered. "Joey, open this door!" The door rattled again; the chair tilted back—but it held.

"Leave me alone!"

He pounded on the door one more time before he gave up. "Okay, but you're gonna have to come out of there sometime."

I stood near the door, every muscle taut, ears strained, but I didn't hear a thing.

I waited for an hour, my head pressed up against the door, listening. When it remained quiet, I risked moving the chair and taking a peek out.

He wasn't there. I snuck carefully around the house, but it was empty.

I got a phone book, looked up the number for the Women's Club, crossed my fingers that it was the right one, and dialed it. After three rings, a voice I didn't know answered. "Yes," I said, trying to sound mature, "it's urgent that I speak to Mrs. Donohue. Is she there?"

The woman said she was. After a few seconds, Mom came on the line.

"Mom, it's me."

"Are you okay, honey?"

I started to cry. I hated it, but I couldn't stop it. "Please come home. Something's wrong with CJ, and Vicki's dead, and I'm really scared, Mom..."

"Oh, honey, I'm so sorry. I'll be right there. Lock the doors and stay in your room until I get home."

"I will."

She hung up. I did what she'd told me to do.

Ten minutes later she was home. She held me while I cried, and then she told me to wait in my room for a few minutes. I didn't want her to leave again, but I knew she was going out to make sure Vicki's body was where I'd said it was.

When she came back five minutes later she was white as a ghost and called the police. She told me she was sure CJ couldn't have had anything to do with such a terrible crime.

I didn't tell her about the blood I'd seen all over him.

Chapter 12

It took the police three hours to show up, and then they were tired and irritable. They told us this was their third murder *today*.

When they asked me how I'd found the body, I told them Debbie had taken me to see it, but that she didn't know anything about it, either.

CJ showed up while they were interviewing Mom and me in the kitchen. He looked clean and wholesome. The distraught performance he gave when they told him who the victim was should have earned him an Academy Award. When they left, they told us only that their best guess was a gang picking off kids as part of some initiation. Maybe Hell's Angels...or gypsies.

They didn't see CJ wink at me as they said that.

After they left, Mom called her sister. Aunt Claire lived in Indianapolis. Her husband was a rich printer, and they had a huge house on the edge of a lake; their own kids were grown and had moved out long ago. I heard Mom saying things like, "I'm not sure how long," and "They don't really know...maybe a gang."

Dad came home late that night, long after I was in bed. I was trying to read a Nancy Drew mystery (or reread it—I'd read it at least four times already) when I heard the shouting start.

That scared me as much as anything that'd happened over the last few days—my folks never fought; or if they did, they did it so quietly that I never knew. Now, though, they were out in the kitchen, both shouting at each other.

I crept to my door, edged the chair aside, and opened it just a crack to listen.

"...and you don't even care," Mom was saying.

"Of course I care," Dad answered. "But I don't know what you think I can do about it—"

"Well, for starters, you can tell me what's going on."

"How would I know?"

They went on in the kitchen for another ten minutes or so, with Dad denying that he knew what was happening (or even that anything was happening) and Mom demanding. Denying and demanding. They were a good pair. I knew they wouldn't resolve anything by the time they moved the fight into the bedroom, but they kept going. Maybe they were as crazy as the kids around here.

I couldn't sleep while they argued in the room next to mine, so I went out to the living room and turned on the TV. There was nothing good on—just the late night talk shows, with a bunch of boring guests. I leaned over to grab the newspaper, thinking maybe I'd read the comics, and then I saw Dad's briefcase on the table next to the paper. It was partly open.

He *never* left his briefcase open. He was probably in the midst of pulling something out of it when Mom started in on him, and he forgot about it.

I'd wondered for years what Dad kept in that case. He always had it with him; sometimes he pulled papers out that he would study, but we weren't allowed to see them, and he always put them back in the case and locked it if any of us came up to him.

There was a report of some kind sticking out of the case. It looked fat and was in one of those same stiff folders that we used for our school reports. My folks were still arguing behind the closed bedroom door, and I knew this might be my only chance, ever, to find out what Dad kept in that case.

I gingerly plucked the report out, half-expecting it to be booby-trapped—like the briefcase might explode, or there'd be poisoned razor blades taped to the back of the report—but nothing happened. I did get a thrill when I opened the cover and saw the word "CLASSIFIED" stamped in red on the first page.

That was about the only word I could understand.

I was pretty good at science, but this was way over my head. There was stuff about "exothermic reactions" and "polymer binders" and velocities and distances. There were mathematical formulae with symbols I didn't even recognize, and names of scientists (including Dad's).

Then I came to something about "test animals." I could follow some of what came next: whatever this was that they'd been working on, when they tested some part of it on chimpanzees, the adults were fine, but "younger subjects exhibited extremely aggressive and even dangerous behavior."

I heard their bedroom door suddenly open, and I jammed the report back in Dad's case, flipping the paper open to the comics.

I tried to look calm as Dad marched into the living room. He looked immediately at his case. Then at me.

"What are you doing out here?" he asked.

I tried to look irritated. "You guys are fighting next to my room. I came out here to get away from it."

It worked. He was abashed enough to give up interrogating me. He did snap the case closed and lock it, but while he did that he said, "I'm sorry about the fight. It's just that...well, things have been kind of stressful at work lately..."

"Gee, Dad," I said before I could stop myself, "are your friends dying at work? Because that's what's been happening to me at home. So I guess stuff's pretty stressful for all of us."

He stopped, and for a second I thought he might come clean or at least apologize. Finally, though, he said only, "Don't stay up all night with the comics." He hefted the case up and returned to the bedroom. A few seconds later, I heard the door close again.

I went back to my room, thinking about what I'd just read in that report. Something—some kind of fuel?—that Dad was working on had made younger chimps act crazy. Had it somehow gotten loose, out of the laboratories and air force bases, and infected kids in the neighborhood? Did the Russians have something to do with this? Was it intentional on their side…or an accident on ours? I thought back on everything that had happened over the last few weeks, starting from Mary Ann Wilson—the first dead girl—and I realized something:

This all started when we thought the moon had blown up, when the smog got even thicker and turned our skies into a perpetual molten yellow. What was it I thought I'd heard Dad say that day?

"This shouldn't have happened."

No, Dad, it shouldn't have, but it did…and I think you know everything about it.

I went to bed trying to figure him out. In my imagination, my dad became like a combination of Ernst Stavro Blofeld and T.H.R.U.S.H. He was a criminal mastermind, a spy overlord, a comic book villain. He was a mad scientist creating a new super rocket fuel that turned young chimps and teenaged humans into killers. And all he had to offer in return was, "This shouldn't have happened."

I hated him.

Maybe I would have felt differently if I'd known that I'd never see him again.

Chapter 13

By morning, I'd decided that I was going to tell Mom about the report in Dad's briefcase. I knew she might be a little mad at me for sneaking it out and reading it, but at this point Mom was my last ally, and the more she knew, the better.

I was out of bed and getting dressed when I heard Mom shouting in the kitchen. "CJ, unlock this right now!"

I finished pulling on my shoes and ran out to the kitchen. To say I was unprepared for what I saw next would be putting it mildly.

Mom was standing by the refrigerator gripping the door handle, and it took me a second to realize that it wasn't just that she was gripping it but that she was *handcuffed* to it.

CJ stood a few feet away, laughing like a crazy man. He dangled the handcuff keys in one hand.

He also wore a gun belt, complete with holstered revolver, around his waist, and had a policeman's cap on his head.

Mom saw me and her eyes got wide. "Joey, get back in your room and lock the door!"

CJ turned and saw me, and his hand moved down to hover near his stolen pistol. "Nah, it's okay, little sister's not gonna do anything stupid, is she?"

"CJ," I said, trying to sound calm and almost pulling it off, "why is Mom handcuffed to the refrigerator?"

"Oh, you gotta love this..." CJ gestured from the fridge to the oven on the other side of Mom. "See, I want her to keep cooking for us, but I don't need her getting in my way. This is perfect, because she can still reach the refrigerator and the stove."

"What if she needs to use the kitchen sink?"

That made CJ frown. "Oh, yeah..." After a few seconds of thought, he brightened. "No problem: I'll get a length of chain and a padlock to replace the handcuffs."

Mom shot me a look that said, *Stay out of his way.*

I tried an offhanded shrug. "Okay. So where's Dad?"

"Who cares?"

I started for my room. "Not me," I threw back over my shoulder. I went into my room, closed the door, crawled up onto my bed...

And just shook.

I didn't know what to do. CJ had a policeman's gun, hat, and handcuffs, and I could only think of one way he could've gotten those things. I'd always counted on Mom to take care of me, but now I might be the one who had to take care of her. But how? Even if I could somehow get the keys away from CJ...could we get to the car in time? Where would we go? Would he shoot at us if he caught us trying to leave?

I finally realized I couldn't think about any of those things. I wasn't going to let myself be paralyzed by fear. I had to do *something*.

I listened for a while, but the house seemed quiet. I opened my door, held my breath, then ventured out to the kitchen.

There was no sign of CJ. Mom was tugging on the handcuffs, trying to pull the handle off the refrigerator, I guess. So far all she'd done was make her wrist bloody.

"Mom..."

She saw me and stopped struggling. "Joey, are you okay, baby?"

I ran up to her, and we had a long hug, her using her one free hand. "I'm fine, Mom. I'm fine."

When we finally pulled apart, I asked, "Where's CJ?"

"He left. I think he went to get some chain."

I looked at the handcuffs. "We've got to get you out of here before that."

Mom shook her head. "I don't think CJ will hurt me as long as I'm still useful. It's you I'm worried about."

"I don't know what to do. I don't think we can call the cops anymore…"

"No, I don't think we can." Mom thought for a minute, then said, "Here's what I want you to do: go across the street and see if Marge can drive you to our bank. I'll write you a check, and you can take my ID—tell them I'm too sick to cash the check myself. Then I want you to go to the airport and take the first flight out to Indianapolis. You're going to stay with your Aunt Nancy."

"Mom, I'm not leaving you—"

"Michaela Jo, don't argue with me on this!" Mom was breathing hard, and I knew better than to say anything back. Besides, she was right about the first part, at least: maybe Marge could help. Maybe she could saw through the chains on the handcuffs. Then we could take Debbie and we could all go somewhere else, somewhere away from my brother and his friends. Somewhere away from the smog.

"Okay. I'll go try Marge."

"Good girl. If you see your brother, just try to avoid him. Okay?"

I nodded, trying to seem braver than I felt. "Okay."

"Love you, baby."

"I love you, Mom."

Then I put on my shoes, pulled my hair back, and stepped out of the house.

Chapter 14

The smog shimmered overhead like a sea of frying butter, and my eyes teared up instantly. I blinked the pain away and raced across the street to Debbie's house, trying to look as inconspicuous as possible. I'd never been so scared in my own neighborhood before. Fortunately there was nobody around, not even a passing car or a distant lawnmower...which was kind of strange.

I walked up to Debbie's front door, took a deep breath, and knocked. Debbie sometimes liked to run into my house unannounced, but I'd never mastered that talent.

After a few seconds, Sandy answered the door. She was completely naked.

At first I just stared; I'd never seen a naked woman up close before, and even though she was still a teenager, Sandy was most definitely a *woman*, with large breasts, broad hips, and furry thatch between her legs. When she saw me staring, she smirked and struck a pose.

"Well, it's Joey the Tomboy. See anything you like, kid?"

I somehow managed to sputter out, "Is Debbie here?"

"Yeah, she's in the dining room with Mom." Sandy burst into laughter. I had no idea why, but I guessed I wasn't going to like the reason, whatever it was.

When Sandy didn't move, I had to edge past her. There was an uncomfortable scent around her—slightly sour and tangy—and she giggled as I wrinkled my nose. "You know what that smell is?"

"No," I said, wishing I hadn't tried to come over here.

"That's the smell of me and your brother *fucking*." She practically spat the last word out, and then laughed again. I felt my face get hot and knew she was laughing at me.

I ran for the dining room, which was just a few feet down the main entry. "Debbie…"

"Oh, hi." Debbie was in the dining room. So was Marge. Marge, in fact, was spread-eagled on top of the dining room table, with long nails driven through the palms of her hands and the arches of her feet, holding her into place. Debbie still clutched a hammer in one hand, and the blood sprayed across her face had long since dried. Marge was unconscious but breathing; her blood had covered a lot of the table's surface and spilled over onto the floor. I remembered the day that table had been delivered; Marge had ordered it out of a Sears catalog and was particularly proud of it.

Behind me, Sandy said, "I'm going back to my room. You girls have fun. Don't do anything I wouldn't do." I heard her door close a few seconds later. I hoped my brother wasn't in her room; or that if he was, he wouldn't come out while I was here.

Debbie turned her back to me and bent over the sideboard. I moved to where I could see what she was looking at: she had all kinds of tools neatly laid out there, like they were the implements for the guests at a fancy dinner party. Butcher knife, paring knife, ice pick, cleaver, hand saw, more nails, and a potato peeler. For some reason, that last one bothered me more than all the others.

"Wow," I said, trying to sound impressed, "guess you must've been pretty mad at your mom, huh?"

Debbie shrugged and picked up a barbecue skewer, eyeing it critically. "Mad? No. Why?"

"Well, you…nailed her to the dining table."

"Oh, that. No, I was just kind of bored."

"Bored?"

Marge groaned slightly, regaining consciousness.

Debbie looked down at her mother dispassionately. "Well, yeah. And you know, she did get in the way a lot of times."

Marge focused on Debbie standing over her, and her eyes streamed. "Debbie, why are you doing this? Why, baby? Why?"

"Why? Because...I can." Debbie raised the hammer and brought it down on the bloodied fingers of Marge's left hand. Marge screamed.

Debbie raised the hammer again, and before I could stop myself I shouted, "Stop it!"

Debbie froze, and the look she turned on me made my blood run cold. "Or what? Or you'll turn your brother on me? Who do you think helped me hold Mom down while I hammered?"

I tried to will my legs to run, to move, to take me out of there, but nothing seemed to be working right—a backwards stagger was the most I could manage. Debbie advanced on me, hefting the hammer. "Y'know, Joey, if I were you, I wouldn't be so worried about anybody else right now..."

I found my strength then, and I ran. Behind me I heard Debbie laughing, then shrieking, "Run, little girl!"

I got home, slammed the front door behind me and locked it, even though I knew CJ had a key. "Mom!"

Mom was where I'd left her in the kitchen, still handcuffed to the fridge but at least not mutilated yet. "Did you find Marge?" she asked.

My mouth went dry, and I couldn't tell her the truth. I swallowed, and then I lied. "Marge is dead."

"Oh my God. Call the police."

"Mom...CJ..."

Mom shouted at me, panicked now. "It's our only chance! We can't just stand here and wait for them to come after us."

"Okay."

I went into the hallway where the phone was, picked up the handset, raised it to my ear—and heard nothing. I stabbed at the little buttons in the cradle a few times, but nothing.

The line was dead.

I went back out into the kitchen. Mom looked at me and knew something was wrong. "What is it...?"

"The phone's out. CJ's probably cut the line."

Mom slumped a little for a few seconds, then called, "Joey, come here."

I did. She put a hand on my chin, tilting my face up to look her in the eyes. "I want you to get on your bike and ride."

I started to protest, "But—"

"No buts. You can outrun anything but a car. Get on that bike, and ride to my Women's Club. Use the phone to call the police, or have one of the ladies drive you to the station."

"I don't want to leave you—"

"I know, honey, but neither of us is safe here like this. If you can get us help, we might have a chance."

"Okay. I'll be back soon."

She smiled proudly at me, and I really loved her right then. "I know you will, sweetheart."

I didn't hug her or say goodbye, because that would have been too much like some last gesture. Instead I just headed right for the garage...

...and the ride of my life.

Chapter 15

I opened the garage door, then went in. I kept my bike near the middle, near some boxes of Christmas decorations and Dad's tool desk, which he never used but kept in perfect order.

I moved the kickstand up, grabbed the handlebars, started walking the bike to the front of the garage—

CJ stood there. "Going somewhere?" He was shirtless, dressed in nothing but shorts and flip-flops.

"Maybe," I said, trying to sound like a sullen kid sister and not a scared-to-death daughter trying to save her mom.

"Like where?"

I tried to roll the bike around him, but he moved to block me. I uttered an exasperated sigh and said, "To the store, okay?"

"For what?"

I glanced across the street at Debbie's house and said the first thing that came into my mind. "A hammer and nails."

"Dad's workbench is right behind you; he's got a hammer and plenty of nails."

"CJ, get out of my way."

"Make me." He planted himself firmly and crossed his arms.

My heart was pounding, my grip on the handlebars was slick with sweat. There was no way I could get past him, and I sure couldn't beat him. Give up and try again later? Hope he didn't decide to bring Debbie over to see my mom next?

"What are you doing, CJ?" It was Sandy, and I'd never been so glad to see a naked woman lounging in her doorway.

"Nothing," CJ shouted back over his shoulder. "I'll be there in a few minutes."

"But CJ," Sandy whined, "I want to fuck *now*."

That did it. CJ turned to call to her, "I'll be right there, baby." Then he looked back at me a last time. "Have a fun ride, dope. Too bad you won't get very far." He walked off to join Sandy; together they went back inside her house.

What did that mean? Why won't I get very far? The street was empty, and CJ was preoccupied. Nobody was around.

He's just being mean.

I got on the bike, desperately hoping that was it, trying to ignore how nervous I was, how much I wanted to turn around and run back into the house...but that didn't seem any safer at this point. So I kept pedaling.

I'd gone about four blocks when I noticed something: the air was cleaner here, the smog lighter. The yellow tint that hovered perpetually over our street was milder here; the sky almost had a hint of blue to it. My lungs and eyes weren't burning as badly.

Then I turned a corner and saw the roadblock.

Maybe fifty yards down, sawhorses had been set up to form a barricade completely across the street. There were trucks parked just behind the sawhorses, big, camouflage-green troop carriers. Men with rifles patrolled around the trucks.

For a second I thought, *They'll help!* Then four rifles lowered and pointed at me. *At me.*

"Halt!" somebody yelled. I didn't even see which one.

I coasted to a stop but didn't get off the bike. "Can you..." I tried to shout for help, but I felt like I was about to throw up, and my voice didn't work. I cleared it and tried again. "Can you help me?"

"You've got ten seconds to turn back."

What? The soldiers hefted their weapons, and I tried not to imagine any trigger fingers getting sweating and slipping. "But I..."

"...nine...eight...seven...six..."

"My mom needs help!"

"...five...four...three...two...one..."

One of them fired a warning shot. The asphalt three feet to the left of me spat up little bits and a plume of dust.

I turned my bike around and pedaled harder than I ever had in my life. I fully expected to feel the bullet hit my back any second—would there be pain, or would I die instantly?

But they didn't shoot. They let me go. And I kept pumping the pedals as fast as I could, until I skidded to a halt in the garage. I just dropped the bike and ran into the kitchen. "Mom!"

I ran up and hugged her, and she comforted me as best she could. "What happened, baby?"

"I tried, I really tried, but there were soldiers, over on El Nido, and they *shot* at me, Mom."

"Oh my God. Are you all right?" She pushed me back to look me over, her movements frantic.

"I'm okay."

We stayed there for a few seconds, then I said, "What are we going to do?"

"I don't know."

And at that moment I realized—maybe for the first time—that my mom was not infallible, that she was helpless, and that it was entirely up to me.

Chapter 16

CJ came in an hour later. He had a long chain and a padlock. He undid the handcuff attached to the refrigerator handle, closed it again, looped the chain through it, and then used the padlock to secure the chain to the handle. Mom could move around now, maybe ten feet, but she was still a prisoner.

As he worked, CJ talked. He said he wanted to have a party at our place tonight. He wanted Mom to cook something nice.

"We don't have anything," she told him.

He laughed. "I'll hunt something up."

Fifteen minutes later he was back. His arms were stained crimson, and he carried a sodden brown paper grocery bag. "See what you can do with this," he said, handing the bag over to Mom.

She reached out and pulled out a mottled red filet so fresh it was still dripping blood. "What...?"

I cut her off. "*Don't*, Mom."

She looked at me...and she knew. She knew what the meat was from...or rather *who*. She stared at it, as the juice ran down her wrists, and then she dropped it. It hit the floor with a wet *splat*. "I...I won't..."

I leapt forward to cover for her. "God, Mom, you dropped it." I picked it up and carried it over to the sink, talking over my shoulder as I washed it off. "We can let it marinate for a while in some of that teriyaki sauce we've still got, then grill it. I think we've still got some onions..."

CJ bought it, or at least decided I was no threat. "Good. I'll tell the gang."

He left.

Mom dropped. Or at least she dropped as far as the chain would let her. I made sure CJ was gone, then knelt by her. "I'm sorry, Joey, I can't do this..."

"You've got to." I took her hands and pulled her back up. "Just until I can figure out how to get us out of here."

When she looked at me, her eyes were haunted. "Did CJ kill Marge?"

"No. Debbie did." That was almost true. I didn't mention that CJ was probably the one who'd thought of the oh-so-clever way to dispose of Marge's leftovers.

"I don't understand...what's happened here?"

"I don't know, Mom. We just need to focus on our own stuff right now. And that means doing what CJ wants for at least tonight."

Mom glanced at the bloody pool the filet had left on the floor. "I can't, Joey..."

I grasped her hands as hard as I could and saw her wince. *"You have to."*

She didn't nod...but she opened the refrigerator, reached in, took a gulp from a bottle of vodka, pulled out a bag of onions, and started chopping.

Chapter 17

Three hours later, CJ had Larry and two other boys I barely knew seated around our big redwood table in the backyard. I was playing waitress, bringing the food out to them, keeping them supplied with drink. They'd shown up with a couple of crates of beer; I didn't ask where they'd found them.

They laid into Mom's cooking with relish. There'd been half a dozen slabs of meat in the bag, and Mom and I had turned ourselves to stone and cooked them up.

"God*damn*, CJ, but your mom can cook," Larry said around a mouthful of rare steak.

I was just setting down the last of the cooked meat when CJ fixed an eye on me and said, "There's only one thing wrong with this dinner: little sis isn't joining us."

The boys all laughed and agreed.

I nearly puked.

"I ate already," I said. It was a bad lie, and CJ saw through it.

"Oh, c'mon, there's always room for a little *housewife*!" His audience roared.

CJ held out a half-finished plate to me. He jabbed a fork in a piece the size of a Ping-Pong ball and put it up to my mouth. The rest stared, waiting.

Larry leaned forward. A trickle of saliva ran out of the corner of his mouth. "Hey, CJ, I'll give ya twenty bucks for your sister."

CJ snickered. "She's *twelve*, man."

Larry's eyes crawled down over my body. "I know."

I was going to end up as Larry's dessert if I didn't do something, so I grabbed the fork CJ held up and bit into the speared portion.

I won't tell you what it tasted like or what the texture was, because I made a deal with myself as I chewed that I would never think about those things. Ever.

Instead I chewed and swallowed and smiled. "Not bad. A little heavy on the tobacco for my taste."

They laughed again, and CJ clapped me on the back as he handed me the plate. "You're all right, kid. Here, you can have the rest."

He turned back to the guys, already forgetting me. I took the plate and walked back into the house. I forced myself to walk slowly and steadily, one foot in front of the other, up for the step that led into the house, right around the corner of the door. I set the plate down on the kitchen counter by the sink.

I ran into the bathroom.

I waited, but I didn't vomit. I even wanted to. I worried that something was wrong with me if I didn't. My stomach roiled, but the food stayed down.

An hour later, CJ and his buddies were all passed out in the backyard, crumpled beer cans in the grass around them. I deliberately dropped a heavy pan in the kitchen to see if it would wake them. It didn't.

Mom watched as I went through the kitchen cabinets until I found what I wanted: her heavy wooden rolling pin. It was solid enough that I had a hard time holding it up long. It was what I needed.

"What are you doing?" Mom hissed at me.

"I'm going to get the keys to that lock," I told her, nodding at the padlock that kept her chained to the refrigerator.

"You can't. CJ keeps them in a pocket.""I know."

Mom looked at the rolling pin and knew what I had in mind. "Joey, he's your brother..."

"I won't use it if I don't have to. And if I have to...I won't kill him, Mom. I promise."

Of course I had no way of keeping that promise. The pin felt heavy enough to kill a giant with. I could've taken out Odd Job with it. But at that moment, after what CJ had made me do (and what Larry *wanted* to make me do), I didn't much care if it killed him or not.

"Joey..."

I didn't answer her. I was already creeping out the back door.

It was a warm night; a glow in one part of the sky told me the moon was full, or nearly so, but it was hidden behind the smog. I paused to let my eyes adjust, then picked my way on tiptoe around the debris.

I passed Larry first; fortunately he was snoring loudly enough to cover any noise I might have made, but the idea of having to walk too close to him still made me shiver. The other two guys were to my right. CJ was to the left.

My brother was sprawled in the lawn on his back, arms thrown out, head tilted to one side. He wasn't a snorer, but his breathing seemed deep and even. I knelt down in the grass beside him and set the rolling pin down, pondering.

Where to start? I might only have one shot at this, so I needed to do it right the first time. Of course if the keys were in a back pocket, I was out of luck. I tried to remember what he'd done with them after he'd locked Mom up, and I was pretty sure he'd shoved them into a front pocket. I was on his right side, that pocket just below me, so it should be easy enough...

He moved beneath me, shifting position slightly to his left.

I froze, fully expecting him to wake up, see the rolling pin, guess my plan, and hand me off to Larry ("*Here, man, I won't even charge you*"). Or maybe they'd just eat me. At least they wouldn't get much meat.

But instead he continued to sleep, and the pocket was now easier to reach.

I took a deep breath and slid my hand out. I rested my fingers lightly on the top of the pocket, and CJ didn't react. I slid my three middle fingers in up to the first knuckle, and he slept on. This was it.

I moved my entire hand into the pocket and gently felt around.

Some papers…two coins…lint…

Keys.

I slid one finger through the key ring, and started to pull, as slowly as possible. Slowly…the keys were coming…slowly…the key ring was appearing now…

The keys came free from the pocket.

They jingled.

I turned to stone.

CJ didn't wake up.

I moved my other hand to form a fist around the keys, muffling any further sound. Then I rose and returned to the house.

As I entered, Mom looked on anxiously. "Did you get them?"

"Yeah…"

I walked towards her, uncurling my fingers from around the keys. I'd gripped them so tightly it hurt to move my fingers.

Shaking slightly, I went through the keys quickly. House key…another large key…a car key I didn't know he had…one padlock key.

I slid it into the lock. It didn't fit.

"What's wrong?" Mom asked.

"I..." I looked at the name of the manufacturer on the key and the one on the padlock.

They were different. This was a key to *another* lock. Probably his school locker or maybe his bike.

"It's not here." I tossed the keys up onto the kitchen counter. "They must be in one of his other pockets."

I walked over to the door. Behind me, Mom called out, "Joey, stay in."

But I was mad. I was going to get those keys no matter what. Even if I had to kill someone.

Even if I had to kill CJ.

I strode across the lawn, less caring if I made noise or not. I'd left the rolling pin behind, and I dropped to my knees by CJ, retrieving the heavy wooden tool. If the key was in his left pocket, there was no way I could reach it without waking him...unless he was already unconscious.

I raised the rolling pin over my head. My muscles shook from the effort. I wanted this all to end, and this was the only answer I could see.

I sat there for seconds, quivering, panting...until the rolling pin fell from my hands into the grass.

I couldn't do it. I couldn't kill CJ.

I picked up the pin and staggered back into the house. I locked the door behind me. Mom watched me with wide eyes.

"I didn't get the key."

"CJ...?"

"He's fine." I returned the rolling pin to its place in the cabinets. I was disgusted with myself. I was weak, a coward, useless.

"Honey...you did the right thing."

"No, Mom, I didn't...because you're still locked up."

Mom nodded at CJ's keys. "You got the keys. And look at it this way: at least he can't get back in without them, can he?"

I hadn't thought of that, and it made me feel better. I ran to the front door to lock it and checked all the windows and the garage. Mom was right—we'd at least bought ourselves a little extra safety.

I still slept that night on some cushions I dragged into the kitchen to be with Mom.

Chapter 18

The sound of something hitting the front door HARD woke me up in the morning. I was groggy, and I couldn't place the sound until it came again, and a third time.

BAM—BAM—BAM-CRACK...

The wood was splintering.

I leapt to my feet and ran out of the kitchen just in time to see an axe blade come through the shattered door. Another chop, and then a booted foot kicked at the boards, and they busted. A hand came through the hole, reaching for the door lock.

A few seconds later, the door was open and Larry was holding the axe as CJ breezed past him.

CJ had a gun. A rifle. I had no idea where it'd come from. We didn't own one.

"You're an idiot," CJ said as he came in, heading for the kitchen, "you didn't really think that you'd be able to keep me out of my own house, did you?"

I bluffed. "What are you talking about, CJ?"

CJ walked up to Mom and hit her in the jaw with the rifle butt. "And *you*—can't you control your own kids?" Mom groaned and sagged as blood burbled out of her mouth.

"CJ, *stop!*"

He spotted his keys on the counter and grabbed them. "These," he said, jangling the key ring in my face. "Cute trick— stealing them while I was sleeping last night."

"I didn't steal them. You left them on the counter, moron."

He stopped and frowned, then shoved the keys in his pocket. I decided to push my advantage. "And you just destroyed our front door. You could've *knocked*, you know."

He looked sheepish. Behind him, Larry said, "I *told* you, CJ—"

CJ cut him off. "Shut up, Larry!"

I gestured at Mom, her jaw already swollen and purpling. "You owe Mom an apology, don't you?"

He looked down at his feet and murmured, "Sorry, Mom."

Mom held up her chained wrist. "I'd accept that apology if you'd let me go."

CJ seemed to consider it. "What would you do if I let you go?"

"Clean up my face, to start with."

Whatever little attention span CJ had briefly mastered was gone—he waved a hand in irritation and turned away. "Ahh, you can do that here. Get her a band-aid, Joey. C'mon, guys, let's go hunting."

They left. CJ didn't even bother to take his keys. I guess nothing on that chain mattered much when rifles and axes could do just as well as keys.

I ran into the bathroom, got rubbing alcohol and bandages and tissue.

"I'm sorry, Mom," I said, as I cleaned blood off her face.

"You did your best, baby." She tried to give me a reassuring smile but winced in pain when her jaw moved.

Chapter 19

Privacy in our neighborhood was a thing of the quaint past, as Debbie proved when she ran in through our shattered front door early the next morning. "Did you hear the great news?"

I was sort of dozing in a kitchen chair, and I looked up, bleary-eyed. "No—what?"

"Your brother said we could go hunting with him today!"

Alarm jerked me up to full wakefulness. "But...what..."

"I know, isn't that great? Come on!" She ran back out.

I looked over at Mom, who nodded after Debbie. "I think you better go."

Mom's face looked bad today, and I didn't want to leave her, but I knew she was right. "Yeah."

I staggered outside. It was just after 8 a.m., and the smog already burned hot and yellow overhead. I blinked as my eyes teared up, then heard Debbie shouting, "What are you bringing?"

Debbie stood in the middle of the street with my brother and his little armed gang. She held the ice pick she'd last used on her mother.

CJ grinned. "She's right, sis, you're almost naked right now."

I didn't like the way Larry looked at me as he laughed.

And I didn't feel well. My stomach was cramped, probably from what I'd eaten last night. I wanted nothing so much as to go back to my room, lie down, and get a few hours of real rest, but I knew that wasn't going to happen. Instead I went into the garage and rummaged until I came up with...

"Oh, nice!" That was CJ, who stood at the front of the garage, admiring the pair of hedge trimmers I held. "Now let's go."

I followed him into the street. He led us north, toward the unseen foothills. "So," I asked, "what's the plan today?"

"Old man Turowski."

Mr. Turowski lived about six houses up. He was a widower with a thick accent and no children. He wasn't directly mean to kids, but he plainly didn't like us. He kept to himself, and I doubt that he'd ever exchanged more than two words with my parents.

"Why Turowski?"

"Why not? Nobody's ever gone in that house, so who knows what he's got in there?" The others murmured agreement.

I didn't ask any more questions. Just stayed at the rear, kept my mouth shut and tried to pretend we were going for a nice visit. Maybe tea and cookies. A beer and barbecue. A Saturday-afternoon ball game on the television.

We reached Turowski's house. It had a neat but unspectacular lawn, just simple grass divided by a concrete walk that led up to the front door. A tan house with a brown door. Some low shrubs. No sound from inside.

They didn't even knock first or try the doorknob—Larry just started chopping.

Wood chips flew as the door started to split. While Larry worked, the others stood by cheering him on, clutching their ice pick, or baseball bat, or rifle, or crowbar tighter. On swing number five, the doorknob flew away and the door swung inward slightly. Larry lowered the axe, grinned back at all of us, then stuck his head around the edge of the door. "Yoohoo—Avon calling—"

BLAM. Something exploded from within the house, and most of Larry's head splattered against us. I wiped away blood and bits of skull, resisting the urge to vomit.

My brother screamed and looked up to see Turowski standing in his front room with a smoking shotgun. He was just shoving another shell in.

CJ didn't give him a chance to finish that; he fired first. The rifle shot hit Turowski in the chest and flung him back and down.

My brother jumped on top of him and began swinging the butt of his rifle into Turowski's head, screaming, "You killed Larry, you bastard, you miserable old rotten stinking Polack bastard!" I head the sickening sound of bone cracking and meat splattering and saw Turowski's head starting to cave in from CJ's blows. The old man's blood was spilling across his wood floor and seeping into CJ's pants where he knelt in it, but he didn't care.

"CJ, he's dead," one of the other guys said.

"I don't care!" CJ did stop then but only long enough to glance back at me and motion at the hedge clippers I'd forgotten I still held. "Joey, cut off his hands."

"Why? He's already dead—"

CJ's scream shocked us all, I think; even the boys flinched. "Because he killed Larry! Now do it."

And I did.

Or at least I tried. I edged around to where I could stand without my shoes slipping in blood, put the blades on either side of one outstretched, dead hand, and pushed. The skin, of course, separated easily; I danced backwards as blood gushed out, but I couldn't cut through the bone. The rest laughed at me as I gritted my teeth and struggled to no avail. Finally CJ made a little grunt of irritation, stood, grabbed the clippers from me, and pressed on the handles, until there was a sound like *shllick*, and the hand was severed. He moved around to the other side of the body and did the same, then handed the clippers back to me. "Good try, kid," he said, and again the other others laughed. Then they tromped off throughout the house in search of plunder.

I stood there holding the clippers, looking down at the blood and carnage, and I realized the strangest thing: except for my slight stomachache, I felt fine. I didn't feel faint or nauseous. I didn't even feel disgust.

I basically felt nothing.

I heard a whoop from the kitchen and went in to see what the commotion was about. CJ was pulling stuff out of Turowski's freezer and putting it into grocery bags. "We struck gold! Old bastard had a freezer full of meat. And here's a little something for you, sis..." CJ tossed me something. I caught it and saw it was an ice cream bar. I tore the wrapper off and devoured it; I hadn't had ice cream in weeks. It made my stomach feel a little better.

There wasn't much else worthwhile in Turowski's place. He'd pretty much lived like a miser, with nothing but a few pictures of his dead wife that made me sad, so I didn't look at them. CJ gave us all bags of food to carry back to our house. It looked like Mom was going to be busy for a while.

As we walked out of the house we stepped over Larry's nearly-headless body, and I was surprised to see that the others ignored it. "CJ," I called after him, as he headed for the sidewalk, "what about Larry?"

"He's dead."

"I know, but...are you going to just leave him here?"

CJ shrugged. "We'll come back for him later. Right now let's get this food to Mom."

He walked away, laughing and kidding with the other two boys and Debbie. I stood over Larry's body, holding my bag of frozen food, feeling cramped and confused and vaguely angry. I hadn't much liked Larry—especially not since last night—but he'd been CJ's best friend for four years, ever since they'd started junior high together. Now he was just a corpse on a dead old man's front lawn, useless and forgotten.

What if I'd been the one shot? Would CJ have just walked away from me?

I finally followed them home. When I reached the kitchen, Mom was already shoving frozen food into our freezer; the gang was out back, celebrating.

There was a fresh, oozing wound on Mom's thigh. "What happened?"

"Debbie thought her ice pick was thirsty. CJ told her to save it."

Dread arced through me; who knew if CJ would stop Debbie the next time.

Mom saw a splatter of blood on my knees. "What happened? Did they—"

"Mr. Turowski shot Larry. Now they're both dead."

"Are you okay?"

"I don't know. I don't feel so good."

I submitted as Mom felt my forehead, decided I didn't have a fever but told me to go rest for a while. Like that was possible.

I used the bathroom first and got another shock when I glanced down at my underwear. There were strange, brown spots there. What were they? Something the smog had done? Was I sick with some new disease? A Russian flu, maybe?

Nervous and embarrassed, I started to tear the panties off, then realized I wasn't about to go from the bathroom to my bedroom with no bottoms on and CJ's friends out there. So I pulled the underwear gingerly back up, re-zipped my shorts, and ran for my bedroom, where I changed everything.

As I pulled on new panties, I realized I should probably tell Mom. Maybe she'd know how to treat it.

I went out to talk to Mom, bringing the evidence with me. Mom was working at the sink, thawing a big roast.

"Mom...I think something's wrong..."

She looked at me, concerned. "What is it, honey?"

I thrust the underwear at her. "I'm sick or something..."

She looked at my panties—and *smiled*. Not a big smile but more of a little melancholy smile. "Oh, Joey, you're not sick."

"I'm not? Then...?"

"You're having your first period."

We'd had "the talk" last year, so I thought I'd been prepared for this...but it wasn't what I expected at all. "But it's brown..."

"It's just dried blood, Joey. It's your first time, and sometimes it's a little spotty at first. Welcome to adulthood."

My head whirled. I grabbed one of the kitchen chairs and sagged into it.

My first period. Then, that meant..."It's not adulthood I'm worried about."

Mom looked at me strangely and then the realization crossed her face. "Oh," she said. After another few seconds, she added, "Oh God."

Adulthood was one thing...but now I was a real teenager. My changes wouldn't be limited to just breasts or boys. My strange new urges might be *really* strange.

After all, I'd cut off a man's hands today and felt nothing.

"You don't have to be like them…" Mom's tone was pleading, desperate. She knew that if I went the way of CJ and all the rest, neither of us stood much chance of surviving this.

"I did something bad this morning…to Mr. Turowski…I mean, I had to—I had to. CJ was there and the others, and Mr. Turowski was already dead—but…it didn't bother me. I'm already starting to be like them."

"You can fight it. You've always been strong, Joey, you don't have to give in…"

I nodded. "I'll try."

But I knew I was lying, because I *could* already feel changes working in me. It wasn't just spotting or cramps; I was angry, and I wanted to take it out on something. I wanted to hit things, make them bleed. I wanted to find Steve again and tell him I wasn't afraid anymore. I wanted Dad to come home so I could kill him…

"Mom, we need to get out of here. I don't think I can make it for long."

"Okay, but…?"

"I'll get the keys from CJ tonight. I promise."

Mom looked at me with doubt written across her face…and I had to stifle the urge to hit her.

Chapter 20

The loot from Turowski's provided another big feast that night; this time Sandy was there, and Debbie, and they let me eat with them. There was still plenty of beer, and I had my first can. It left me reeling and burping after, but it also helped calm me down a little.

After the dinner, CJ hooked up an extension cord and lugged a phonograph out to the patio. He put on Rolling Stones records and Sandy danced while everyone else cheered her on. Her dance turned into more of striptease; by the time it was over she was mostly naked, and the guys were playing with her like an oversized doll, each one kissing and fondling her before passing her on.

Watching left me both electrified and disgusted. Below the waist, I wanted to be Sandy; above, I thought she was nothing but a stupid girl who deserved whatever she got.

CJ and one other boy had their shirts off already, but they were all still drinking; when the first one fell back in the grass unconscious, I knew the rest would follow soon. Sandy was next, and CJ didn't seem to care that she wasn't awake; he fell on her and started grinding against her. But before he got anywhere, he rolled to the side and was out instantly.

In fifteen minutes they were all gone, snoring or quietly slumbering. This was my chance.

As I got the rolling pin out again, Mom whispered to me, "Joey, even if you get the keys...how will we leave? You said they shot at you..."

"It's okay, Mom, I've got something else in mind." I put the pin down, grabbed a canvas knapsack from the hallway closet and put together a bag of stuff I thought we might need: two flashlights, a canteen of water, a knife, Mom's billfold with some money, and her checkbook.

"Do you think you'll be able to walk?"

She nodded grimly.

"Okay. Be ready."

She didn't say anything else as I grabbed the rolling pin, slid past the door and out into the night.

I was less cautious this time, because I'd stopped caring if I had to hit anyone. All I wanted were the keys. They were my one shot at getting away from the desires that were starting to crowd into my head.

I found CJ near Sandy and knelt beside him. He was flat on his back, but Sandy was on his left, so I positioned myself on his right, knowing I'd have to reach over him. Keeping the rolling pin in my left hand, I extended my right, reaching, lowering, just resting on the pocket's rim—

"Cute, sis—very cute."

I flinched and drew back like I'd been burned. CJ was awake and looking at me, although he otherwise hadn't moved yet. I saw the moonlight glint off his bared teeth. I didn't say anything.

He laughed softly, then said, "C'mon, twerp, we both know you haven't got it in you, at least not yet. You're still just a kid."

"CJ—you're an idiot."

Then I hit him.

Chapter 21

None of the others stirred, and I had no idea if I'd killed CJ or just knocked him out. Frankly, I didn't really care; I only wanted those keys.

I found them in his left front pocket. I ran into the house and held them out before Mom. "Got 'em."

"CJ...?"

"I had to hit him."

I undid the cuff around Mom's wrist, and she rubbed it painfully as she asked, "Is he...?"

"I don't know. I just know we have to go—NOW."

Mom stumbled and winced as she walked; a few days of being kept prisoner, burdened with six feet of chain and no way to sit or stand comfortably, had taken a toll on her. "Are you sure you can you walk?"

"I'll be okay."

I picked up the canvas bag and eyed her. "We may have to hike a couple of miles."

"Won't they have all the streets blocked?"

"We're not taking a street." I nodded out the back. "We're going through the wash."

Mom frowned. "The wash...?"

"I figure it might be the only thing they've forgotten to block off. There are ladders leading down into it every quarter mile or so. We just have to scale the fence, find one of the ladders, and climb down. Then we should be able to follow the wash south for a few miles to get past the roadblocks."

She looked pale, but nodded, resolute. "Okay, let's try it."

The first part was maybe the scariest for Mom: picking our way through the failed orgy. She wanted to stop and examine CJ, but when Sandy moaned (and I hissed), she gave up and tiptoed as quickly as possible to the back gate. As I opened it, I cursed its squeaky hinges…but none of CJ's sleeping gang reacted. I held it open as Mom stepped through, closed it as quietly as possible, and led the way along the dirt trail.

In the distance I could see the orange glow of flames, and I knew that one of the houses that backed onto the dirt road was on fire. It would block our way, and we might be in trouble if there was no ladder into the wash between us and the burning house. But there was a (locked) gate in the chain-link fence just ahead, and I hoped there would be a ladder located there.

Mom had a little trouble negotiating the fence. The wound in her thigh slowed her down, especially when it started bleeding again through the bandage I'd wrapped around it; but I finally managed to help her over. Sure enough, there was a ladder right there. I descended first, so I could test it; it was solid, and we both climbed down with no problem.

At that point we switched on the flashlights and started to hike. It hadn't rained in months, and the wash was bone dry. (At least we didn't need to worry about being swept away in some sudden rush of water.) Once we heard screaming and shouts overhead, so we switched off our lights and hugged the wall, trying to make ourselves as invisible and small as possible. The voices passed directly over us, and then vanished into the distance. The only words I made out were, "…God damn it, I'm going to kill him when I find him…"

Our flashlight batteries gave out after an hour, and we rested for a while, our backs against concrete, sharing the canteen. I rewound Mom's thigh bandage, and I knew it hurt when she tried to smile at me. We finally got to our feet and continued on. We heard gunshots once, but they seemed at least a block away. We kept going.

We walked until Mom said she had to stop. At that point we just squatted down and waited for dawn.

When it was light, I told Mom to wait while I checked everything out overhead. We'd camped near a ladder, which I climbed now.

We'd come out near a major intersection—I wasn't sure where it was, but there was normal traffic, and stores were nearby.

We'd made it.

I went back for Mom, helped her up the ladder and over the fence, and together we found a phone booth. As Mom used it to call a cab, I looked up into the sky and realized:

There was no smog...or at least the smog here was light and pale, none of the canary-colored muck I'd grown accustomed to seeing.

And I could feel it, too. I was worried about CJ again. I felt shame for what I'd done to Turowski. And I wanted nothing so much as to be a million miles away from here.

I'd escaped the smog.

Epilogue

The cab took us to Mom and Dad's bank, where Mom withdrew enough money to buy us plane tickets to Indianapolis. A day later, we were living with Aunt Nancy and watching reports on the six o' clock news about the San Diablo quarantine. They called it a flu outbreak. They said thirty people had already died from the disease.

I tried not to remember what had happened to Marge, and Larry, and Mr. Turowski, and Matt's father, and all the rest.

A month later the quarantine was lifted. Order was restored. CJ, it turned out, was fine. I wondered how big a goose egg I'd given him.

He stayed in California.

Mom spent a lot of time on the phone with Dad, who begged us to come home. She answered him by filing for divorce. He didn't contest it.

We settled into life as Midwesterners. I didn't really like it at first—the winters were too cold, the summers humid—but at least there was no smog...or teenagers who wanted to kill and eat their own mothers.

Debbie and Sandy had both survived as well. Sandy ended up marrying Steve, who never became a rock star. Debbie ran off to San Francisco; the last anyone heard of her, she was turning tricks as an underaged hippie chick in Haight-

Ashbury, with an arrest record that included numerous drug-related and assault charges.

Mom and I got pretty used to visits from government men in plain black suits. They asked us what we knew about what'd happened in San Diablo; we lied and told them we couldn't remember. It'd been a terrible flu bug.

Mom's wounds healed, and she gave up drinking.

I talked to Dad a few times on the phone. Once I asked him if he'd been the one who'd finally cleaned out the smog. He told me he didn't know what I was talking about. After that, I got cards from him for my birthday (he never got the date right) and Christmas, but after a few years even those stopped.

It's been a long time now since 1965. I've gotten used to being an adult, although I've never had children of my own. Call it a trust issue. It's hard to share the popular image of innocent tykes when you've seen an adolescent girl you used to like tearing apart her mother.

Instead, I went to work for my uncle's printing company. It turned out I had a minor talent for graphic design and layout. I still read comic books from time to time, although nowadays they're called graphic novels.

CJ has fared better than I have; he's the CFO of a Fortune 500 tech company now. He has a gorgeous trophy wife, three sons, and a mansion in Malibu. One of his kids recently got in trouble at school for bullying. CJ made a large donation to the school's athletics program, and the trouble conveniently vanished. Most people still like my brother; those who don't can be easily bought off.

I don't see him often. When I do—maybe at the holidays, maybe every other year—I smile and pretend I'm happy...but the truth is, every time I look at him, I see a teenaged brother who forced me to mutilate the corpse of a man he'd just slain. I know we were all affected by something, and maybe if I'd come of age earlier, I would have been just as bad...but I remember making choices, even while the smog was working its way through me.

In my pensive moments, I try to remember 1965 before the moon blew up and the smog came, when my brother was just one of the teenagers out on his front lawn on a summer evening, listening to the latest hit record on a transistor radio. I try to remember how we had fun, how we laughed when he put a cricket in my bed...but no matter how hard I try, it doesn't blot out the bad memories that came after. The blood, the sex, the killings. I've spent my life since trying to forget. So far I've been unsuccessful.

I guess I can't get no satisfaction.

The End

Lisa Morton is a screenwriter, a novelist, a short story writer, and a world-renowned Halloween expert. Her fiction works include *The Castle of Los Angeles* (winner of the Bram Stoker Award for First Novel), *The Lucid Dreaming*, and *Monsters of L.A.* 2013 sees the release of her second novel, *Malediction*, and the paperback release of her Bram Stoker Award-winning *Trick or Treat: A History of Halloween*. She lives in North Hollywood, California and online at www.lisamorton.com

Baggage of
Eternal Night

JournalStone's DoubleDown Series, Book II

By
Eric J. Guignard

JournalStone
San Francisco

JOURNALSTONE
YOUR LINK TO ARTISTIC TALENT

JournalStone books may be ordered through booksellers or by contacting:

JournalStone
www.journalstone.com
www.journal-store.com

The views expressed in this work are solely those of the authors and do not necessarily reflect the views of the publisher, and the publisher hereby disclaims any responsibility for them.

ISBN: 978-1-940161-01-3   (sc)
ISBN: 978-1-940161-17-4   (hc – limited edition)
ISBN: 978-1-940161-02-0   (ebook)

Library of Congress Control Number: 2013941614

Printed in the United States of America
JournalStone rev. date: September 6, 2013

Cover Design: Denise Daniel
Cover Art: Alan M. Clark
Edited by: Norman Rubenstein

Endorsements

"Wonderfully weird! Detroit may be gone, but in Eric J. Guignard's Baggage of Eternal Night the majesty that was Detroit so long ago is found again. Guignard writes with an effortless flow that feels so natural, so easy, that I couldn't help but feel I was sitting next to him, listening with rapt horror at the tale he spun. Read this, right now. You will not be sorry." — **Joe McKinney**, Bram Stoker Award-winning author of *Dead City* and *Inheritance*

"Eric J. Guignard is a brilliant writer, and *Baggage of Eternal Night*, his debut work of long fiction, pays off the promise of his early stories, tenfold. The prose is vivid, the characters richly drawn, and the pages seem to turn themselves. Do yourself a favor— don't miss this!" — **Peter Giglio**, *author of* Stealing Night *and* Lesser Creatures

Dedication

Dedicated to my family;
We're all collectors of something.

Thanks also to Lisa, Chris, and Norm
for inspiring me.

Chapter 1

I want to tell you about Joey Third.

You probably never heard of Joey before, but at one time in the early 1950s he was a big-shot gambler in the underworld circles of Chicago and Detroit. Joey Thurston was his real name, but *Joey Third* is the name some wise guy called him on account of there being three different Joeys gambling one night in Little Louie's Den. After that, the name just stuck.

Joey and I became good friends. I didn't get to know him until after his poker days were over. I wouldn't have associated with him in those backroom circles anyway; those were the tables run by gangsters like Joseph Zerilli and Angelo Meli, men who could make you vanish if you laughed at the wrong joke or they didn't like the color of your tie. But by 1959, Joey had quit with the cards. Seemed that when he lost at poker, he really lost big. And when he won...well, he still lost. After a night of straight aces, two mucks accused him of cheating and broke every bone in his left hand with a framing hammer. I don't believe Joey ever cheated—the times I knew him, he would return a gold watch to a man that dropped it on the street. I think those mucks that busted his hand were just sore losers. That, or their bosses were.

Anyway, how I met Joey was at the baggage auctions. Joey may have soured on cards, but he was a gambling man at heart. I began to recognize him at places like Roman's and the liquidation house on 23rd. I got used to seeing him waving that crippled hand of his up in the air, those ruined fingers askew like the twisted legs of a dead spider. Joey had an affable presence about him, a sense that, whether he was joking or irritable or even plain silent, one could still find companionship just by standing next to him. He was a genuine people-person. I won a few auctions over him, and he won a few over me, and pretty soon we'd get to drinking a couple mugs afterward, bearing a bond of baggage gambling.

Now, in case I'm getting ahead of myself, let me explain what a baggage auction is, for those of you not around during the war in the Koreas. These auctions are for pieces of luggage that go unclaimed at all the big hotels. Maybe the guests forgot about the baggage. Maybe folks got locked up, or they didn't pay the bill...maybe they died. The bags are sold off unopened to the highest bidder. You never know what you're going to find inside, but with a little education and experience, you get pretty good at guessing. A big, frumpy carpet bag with paisley print on it likely contains some old marm's stockings and brassiere. A scuffed attaché case might contain makeup or the display merchandise of a traveling salesman. A midsize valise, plain in color, but from a high-end manufacturer—well, those are the best to go after. More often than not, you'll find a gentleman's vanity or lady's jewelry inside. The first time I competed in an auction, I bid one dollar and won a dented footlocker speckled on the front by dark stains. Inside was an envelope stuffed with ten fifty-dollar bills. After that, I was hooked for life.

The tale I want to tell you about Joey Third involves a leather suitcase he won at a baggage auction. I want to tell you about what was *inside* that suitcase.

It all began late on a Thursday afternoon in the midst of July. I remember that day because the Tigers had taken an awful pounding by the White Sox for three days in a row. The whole city just seemed to slump at that, as if every building and car were inflatable and air slowly leaked out from the seams. People were in a foul mood and the summer heat didn't help none. The baggage auctions were normally a hoot for Joey and me both, but our hearts didn't seem to be in it that day.

The auctions were a weekly event, every Thursday afternoon, and that day it was held offsite in a distribution warehouse that doubled as a union hall. There weren't even chairs to sit on. We just stood in a large group, sweating and small-talking. Most of the guys in there knew each other—we all traveled to the same auctions the way you would follow horses at the tracks. We had our favorite auctioneers and our favorite hotels that the luggage came from. Today wasn't much different, except we were in the warehouse rather than a lodge or liquidation house.

Joey and I worked our way over to Ray Galler, a friend from the north side of town who owned a couple consignment shops. Ray was also an art and collectibles dealer who bought anything of value that we won. Between his stores and his private dealings, Ray could find a buyer for just about anything, if the price made sense. He was only a few years older than us but twice the hustler. I didn't make a lot of money from the auctions or races or my other gambling ventures—I also ghostwrote political editorials to pay the bills—but to Ray, the auctions were a way of life.

He had a habit of snapping his fingers when he spoke, as if the words hid a secret beat only he could hear. He snapped away. "Charlie, Joey, what do ya say? Anything lookin' hot?"

The bidding started at five o'clock, but you were allowed to preview the closed baggage for an hour before.

"Your eyes are as good as mine," Joey said.

"What do you think of the big steamer trunk over there?"

"I saw it," I replied. "Had nice locks, solid brass and polished. Somebody took good care of it."

"Could be some nice artwork inside," Ray said.

"Or Grandma's family photos," Joey replied. "Bet it wasn't used for nothing but a hope chest, filled with baby clothes."

"But why would someone cart it along to a hotel if that's all it held?" I asked.

"People bring strange things with them when they travel. You should know that by now."

Joey was right; I did know. The wonder was endless when it came to trinkets that people found valuable. I once knew a man who was destitute and homeless, but who carried with him a large box of baby rattles wherever he went. Those rattles meant the world to him, but to anyone else it was a collection of pastel-colored crap that sounded like shattering glass whenever he moved.

The auctioneer arrived and announced it was time to start bidding. Before you could whistle, the first suitcase was carried in by a porter and the auctioneer jumped right into the whole spiel. He was country-fat—the kind raised on gravy and hog—and his teeth stuck out as if his mouth caught fire and every chomper tried escaping in different directions. But his voice was molten honey, burning hot and pouring from between those screwy teeth in a flood of sweet words.

"First up open bid, one dollar for the green soft case, do I hear one? One! Over there, do I hear two? Two! Over there, now three, give me three, three dollars for the soft case. Three! The man in the back, going four, now four, do I hear four? Four! Man in the green coat, going five, now five, going five once, going five twice. Sold! Four dollars, man in the green coat."

The first case sold in about seven seconds, and one porter set it aside, while a second porter carried in the next item, a canvas tote bag.

As a matter of habit, Joey and I bid the minimum—one dollar—on just about anything, and the bids increased depending on our interest. The experienced bidders let the price rise on its own, as it didn't make sense to inflate the market right away on used items. That's how you could tell those who knew what they were doing against the dabblers, anyone who was anxious or inexperienced. Ten items into the auction, and one guy outbid everyone by yelling out forty bucks right away for a leather portmanteau. That suggested maybe it was his own to begin with and he needed it back. I used to think a sudden high bidder knew there was something valuable inside an item and tipped his hand the way a guy over-bets at cards when he's got a royal flush. I went up against a couple of those schleps in the past and won, only to find the case filled with stockings and rotting knickers. I lost a lot of money and couldn't get the smell from my nose for a week. You just never can figure out the motivation behind some people's bidding decisions.

As it was, we never did find out what was in that portmanteau, or if it was worth the money he over-bid. It was house policy—and common sense—that you opened the bags privately, off premises. There were two reasons for this: first, the auction houses didn't want winners to just skim the contents and leave the empty luggage lying around for the proprietor to have to dispose of. Second was for the safety of the winners; you didn't want to open a case in front of hoods when a trove of valuables might be stuffed inside.

That auction, Joey and I each won a couple of suitcases and purses. Just before we were set to leave and after the auction had ended, one of the porters ran up dragging a heavy leather case that had somehow been set apart from the others. The auctioneer announced there was another item, but most of the bidders were already leaving, and the rest had spent all their money. Joey won that last item with his default opening bid of one dollar.

Afterwards, we went back to our apartments. Joey and I lived in the same building, me on the sixth floor and him on the fourth, of a complex that once had been a swanky hotel during the thirties, but since then changed owners and suffered renovations, so that linoleum and *Vacancy* placards overlaid the memory of its glitz. *Les Deux Oies*. That was its name—French for "The Two Geese." I'm told the hotel was originally owned by Hollywood Jews, designed by Swedes, built by Italians, and then christened in French. Maybe that's why it never succeeded: the national *melting pot* philosophy never seemed to fare well when it came to local business economy. Folks get confused, and a hotel ends up being called "The Two Geese."

We elected to go to my apartment, as it was filled with slightly less leftover luggage than Joey's. That's the burden of the auctions—we brought things in faster than we could dispose of them. Piles of teetering boxes and empty suitcases pressed up against the walls of our homes, nearly as high as the ceiling, placed where other men might erect bookcases or cabinets. Containers of shot glasses were stacked on cartons of bowling shoes that sat upon cases of screwdrivers that all listed precariously above egg crates filled with gloves and flashlights and tubes of artist's oil paints. Then, that was bookended on one side by the props from someone's Coney Island magic show and on the other side by a locker filled with the equipment of a man who scaled Mount Everest. Neighboring bulwarks were composed of magazines, German steins, fishing lures, candles, cufflinks, sports gear, batteries, bottle caps, typewriters with missing keys, ornamental Easter eggs, jars of face cream, wood carvings, cameras without film, and a thousand other items I meant to inventory but never got around to.

I brought out a couple of Stroh's beers, and Joey and me settled down on my living room floor to open what we won today.

It was like Christmas between us. We took turns opening each piece of luggage one-at-a-time, so as to share the excitement of its contents with each other.

"Lookee here, Charlie," he said as he popped the latches on a pink-striped carton. "I got a fancy evening gown. Maybe you have something I'll trade you for. This would make a nice gift for your lady friend to really impress her."

"Keep it. I've got a dozen in every color already stored in the back of my closet."

He laughed. "Yeah, I've got more broads' clothes than I do of my own. If anybody looked in my closet, they'd think I was a fruit."

I chuckled at that. Both our apartments looked like secondhand stores, filled with the junk of Detroit.

It was my turn, so I unlatched a valise. "Couple wigs in here to match your dress. A bunch of medications for stomach illness. Pair of Bibles. I suppose you need a backup in case the devil clips the first copy from you."

"The Gideons would be proud."

When you get to be middle-aged like we were, there're not a lot of thrills left in life, but opening the cases made us feel like excited children, exclaiming over what was inside. Sometimes we moaned over the contents, as a child does when finding a lump of coal in his stocking. Other times we shrieked with rapture, like the time Joey won a bid and found a stash of ruby-lined gold rings hidden inside, or when I found the polished old sword and pistol of a conquistador wrapped in gingham cloth at the bottom of a crate.

Today, it was mostly moans. Our other luggage held old men's shirts, dirty britches, hair tonic, and some nice shoes that were too large for either of us.

"Not even Ray's going to want any of this," I said. "I think we got skunked."

"Speak for yourself. I've still got that left-behind case that I won. It's old and heavy, and I'm feeling good about it." He held his hands over the case, as a mystic might do in order to discern its hidden power. "I'm hoping someone left bricks of gold inside."

Joey's last case *did* look old, and it looked European, like the kind of luggage shown on posters for luxury cruise liners that crossed the Atlantic. The large frame was wrapped in brown leather and crossed with a pair of double-stitched belts. Its handle appeared to have been carved from a hard, white substance like ivory, and there were similar white stones with a greenish hue embedded along the edge of the case where it would open apart.

"Never seen a piece of luggage quite like this," he said.

The suitcase was the size of two couch cushions stacked on top of each other and fastened by a thick bronze padlock overlaying the latches. "Don't suppose a key came with it?"

We owned a hammer and a set of chisels for breaking apart locked baggage. More often than not, however, we didn't need to use them. Joey maintained a collection of lock picks and the knowledge of how to use them. He selected a hook pick and twisted it around inside the lock for a few moments with his good hand. It clicked apart. Joey tossed the padlock aside and opened the case.

Inside was a gramophone, the old type of record player that was popular during turn-of-the-century years, with the horn speaker like a funnel that the sound came out from. I'd only seen units like that in the city museum and antique stores.

"Maybe we can invite some dolls over and have a party with this," he said.

I thought of my girlfriend, Gail, who dressed nice and smelled good all the time and kept her home spotless. She hated coming over to visit me here. 'Filthy,' was the word she most frequently used to describe my living conditions.

"Gail's not too keen on carousing where stacks of boxes might topple onto her," I said.

"I didn't say *which* dolls to invite."

"Always causing trouble, ain't ya?"

Joey grinned. His lips pursed together and his cheeks rose, reminding me of a little boy who might suggest we sneak a sweet from the confectioner.

"Anyway, it probably doesn't work, it's so old," I said.

"And maybe it does," he replied. I couldn't tell if he was ribbing me or really *was* hoping to throw an impromptu bash. I hated people visiting whom I didn't already know. Gail was admittedly right in the description of my living conditions, and it embarrassed me.

Joey pulled the record player out and lifted the horn into place. The base of the player was rich-grained wood, sized about one foot in all dimensions. The turntable and horn were brass. A handle, like the crank of an old car, punched out from one side.

"I remember my grandmother used to have one of these in her sitting room," I said. "A real lively bird she was, playing music every afternoon, recorded by the pianist from her church."

"My grandma just whipped me with a stick of elm if the chickens weren't fed by sunrise."

"Is that why you're so damaged?"

Joey slapped me on the shoulder, and his chuckle made the room feel twice as large. "Here's cheers to grandmas, though I'd rather be cheering to some younger dames." He popped the cap off another Stroh's and downed half the bottle.

He continued. "I'll get this working and you'll either have a shindig with me, or I'll make you listen to piano gospel all night."

"Let's see what else you've got in there first."

Inside the old case were two more boxes, each with a flip lid, and I opened them.

Joey fingered through one. "Looks like there's quite a library of records in these boxes to mix it up. I suppose it's hoping too much for some Perry Como or The Shirelles."

Between the two boxes, I estimated there were about forty or fifty albums, each a flat black disc of wax. None of them were identified by labels, and each disc appeared identical; thick and handmade, with deep grooves set wider than the stereophonic vinyl albums of today.

"What do you make of this?" I asked and pointed at one of the boxes. A series of lines in strange writing like Eastern European characters were sketched in ink, followed by numbers, as if a series of ledger entries.

Joey set the gramophone on a chair and began winding the mechanical crank. Old record players worked like music boxes; the sound was produced through manual effort, without electrical amplification. "I don't know," he said, "but let's hear what they've got to say."

I pulled out a record, and Joey set it on the turntable. He released the crank. At first there was silence. I took another swig of Stroh's.

It started off with a scratching sound, like a hen trying to dig around in a yard made of sheet metal. Then some old-timey horn blew the most melancholy notes I ever heard, and that was followed by something that could have been a clarinet that played even more doleful than the horn. I heard a tinkling which might have been a piano and something else I couldn't even guess at, that sounded like someone with molasses in their throat breathing fast into a paper sack. If that was what music sounded like in the early nineteen hundreds, I understood why the country soon fell into a Depression.

"Makes me want to stab ice picks through my ears," Joey said.

The instruments played for half a minute in choral rhythm, following a series of timed beats and then crashed together in a burst of clatter, before slowing back down again. I once visited New Orleans in my younger days and heard the slow jazz marches of a funeral procession. If I had to make a comparison, this record sounded closest to that, only the instruments here were off-key and played together like children experimenting with contraptions found in the city dump.

And then a voice spoke.

Or, rather, chanted. Joey and I looked at each other. I immediately felt nauseous, the way castor oil curdles in your guts, and I saw Joey felt the same. The voice was a man's and he spoke in slow solemn words, the intonations seeming to reverberate throughout my room in low bass rumbles. The words were unfamiliar, but emotions dripping with wet fog somehow filled each syllable, and my head swooned.

Vkhodite. Vkhodite. Vkhodite.

Ne zaderzhivat'sya v kholodnyy i temnyy, ho prisoyedinit'sya ko mne v svet navsegda.

Vkhodite. Vkhodite. Vkhodite.

The sensation changed and the nausea reversed until euphoria touched me. The words repeated over and over and each became a finger rubbing inside my temples, massaging my brain. The world seemed to shift slightly beneath me; shadows grew longer from behind the stacked baggage, and my thoughts slowed. I felt relaxed, like slipping under the water of a warm bath.

I lost track of time as the chanting words repeated themselves. I descended further into the bath, floating free in a stillness that must be like what an embryo experiences as it develops in the womb.

Though I felt good, almost weightless, I sensed something was out of line.

"Turn it off," I finally said to Joey. He looked at me from far away, and his eyes were heavy-lidded, as I felt mine must have appeared to him. His expression though was wan as if he couldn't fathom who spoke, much less act on my directions.

I had to focus on the movements in my arm, but I willed myself forward. The record must have been playing for at least ten minutes, yet the needle still played in the first groove of the disc, as if it had only begun. I lifted the needle, and the sudden silence was like the slap of a cold hand.

Joey's eyes focused, and he leaned back to lie on the floor. "Mama, I feel like I just came off a three-day bender."

"I feel like someone slugged me in the temple."

He rolled over and grinned. "Sure beats Grandma's church music."

I couldn't agree with that; I thought I'd rather listen to a hundred hours of piano hymnals than just a second more of that strange man's chant. His voice—those words—echoed in my mind.

Vkhodite. Vkhodite. Vkhodite...

The words were unfamiliar, yet they *spoke* to me. I couldn't understand them, but I believed it sounded like a modern language, if only some backwards Baltic dialect. The speaker's articulation was flat, void of intonation, and the rhythm was like breathing. In fact, I felt that it somehow crept *inside* my breaths while I listened, the same way it climbed into my thoughts.

"Hey, Charlie, wake up." Joey snapped his fingers at me. "I said, 'What do you think the record was saying?'"

I looked at him, realizing part of me still drifted away. "I don't know, but it sure wasn't whispers of sweet love."

"Maybe this is some sort of hypnosis used on prisoners during the first World War. That'd make sense, right? I mean, if you wanted to drive someone crazy, just flick this on all night long."

"Maybe so," I said. "It bugged me out right away."

Joey nodded and we were quiet, each looking at the gramophone. If he were like me, Joey had to wonder at what exactly he brought home that night.

He lifted his crippled hand, looking at each finger one-by-one. "You know what else, Charlie?"

"I couldn't guess."

"I imagined I was flying," he said. "Does that make sense? While that played, I felt like my body didn't weigh anything and I lifted from the earth. I mean, I knew it was wrong, but I couldn't control it. I just drifted up into the stars."

"Funny," I said. "I kind of felt the same, like I was floating free in a warm bath."

"What do you think these records are worth?"

"A trip to the city dump."

"Get outta here! I've never encountered anything like this before. That's got to account for something. You think Ray will take a look at it?"

"Maybe. Or maybe we should just scrap the thing. We seem to agree there's something off about it."

Joey either ignored my comment or wasn't listening. "Ray knows antiques. Of course, this being a foreign language might throw him. I sure wish I knew what it said."

"Aw, hell, I know a guy who's into languages." I said. I thought Joey was probably right about it having some sort of value. Of course, when it came down to it, the stranger an item, the more value it commands. "Real sharp fella. He's a Hungarian that runs a book store I used to live by, about as cultured a mind as you're going to find in these parts. I'll bring him the player in the morning and ask what he makes of it."

"Just bring him a couple of the albums. I'm going to listen to some of the others on my own, see what else is on here."

"What's he going to do with records and no player to put it on?"

"It's 1963. Everyone's got a record player."

I shrugged, and Joey packed up the gramophone and his other winning baggage. We said our goodnights, and he walked out the door of my apartment. As soon as he left, the room felt a little colder, a little smaller.

1963 was half over and I felt old and slow, as if the year sped past, shooting clouds of dust at me as it blew by. I remembered that I once had a plan for life, a direction, but now I just lived for the day. Making bets and going to the auctions was always a hoot, but part of me felt that I settled for something I wasn't meant for. Truth was, I always wanted to live in the city, but I also thought I would get a fancy job in business or law, drive a big car, and travel to Europe. I made it to the city, but I found regular work didn't suit me. Getting chained to a desk for ten hours a day made me think of stories about men that drowned in quicksand: once they start sinking, it's harder and harder to get out and after a certain threshold is passed—just above the naval on a full-grown man—escape is impossible. They can only scream and flounder and know death is cruel and inevitable. To me, that's what every day at an office job was like.

I got out in time, but I also lost my dream. I might have given up and moved back to the warmer climes of my native Kentucky, if I hadn't met Danielle. We got engaged quick, ten years ago, and then I caught her in bed with a jockey...a jockey I had bet against earlier that day at the track and who went against the odds, winning in the final lap. Within five hours, I lost my money and I lost *her*. I stood a foot taller than that horse-riding bastard, and when I caught them doing the wild mamba in bed I called him out and laid all my force into a crack against his jaw. He barely flinched, and then he landed an uppercut that knocked me clean out. When I woke, they both were gone. To this day, all I can figure is that he was experienced with having wronged men hit him and had trained to take punches.

Either that, or I hit like a pansy.

After Danielle, I met Gail, whom I've come to love like no other. If not for Danielle, I would have proposed marriage to Gail long ago. As it was, I couldn't bring myself to do it. Too much pain and betrayal associated with the custom. Gail kept me rooted in reality; she worked the regular business job I couldn't hold, she had the big car and the future. I wished someday to make an honest woman out of her, though I knew deep down she deserved better than me. I regularly expected her to cut me loose.

How many Stroh's did I drink? I thought of Joey and Danielle and Gail and all the people from my life speaking to me from a record. And there, tiny amongst the towers of luggage and reminiscences, I faded into night's dreams.

Chapter 2

The next day I drove to Vic's Books in one of the city's historic quarters lining the Detroit River's north bank. Vic was west of the Ambassador Bridge that connects to Canada, and every time I drove past, I thought of how many forlorn people took a quarter mile walk either way, hoping to start life over in a new country, only to find out that it's the same troubles everywhere.

I arrived at the shop and parked in front. Vic's Books was a small glass-faced square in the shopping district, one of many like an assemblage of bright children's blocks laid in line.

Carrying three of Joey's records wrapped in a pillowcase, I pushed through the front door. A small bell announced my entrance. Inside were cases of paperbacks and clothbound volumes crammed into every space. The musty smell of aged paper filled the room like a presence—a good presence—and I was reminded of lazy afternoons lounging in my grandfather's study reading childhood adventures in exotic lands.

There were no other customers in the store, and I made my way through towering aisles of ancient tomes and Harlequin tales until I reached the back, where Vic sat reading the *Detroit Times* and smoking a frayed cigar.

"Charlie," he said without looking up. "Been too long since you stopped by. Never too busy to read, son."

"I read."

"The pony stats don't count." He looked at me over the edge of gold-rimmed focals, the kind with a piece of twine that circles your head and attaches to the arms like a necklace.

"All right, I'll buy something if that's what you want," I said.

"Of course that's what I want. I run a business don't I?"

"I said I'll buy something." I shrugged.

He shrugged back.

"And it's nice to see you, too," I added.

"Hey, I'm just giving you a hard time."

"Same old Vic. You age, you don't change."

He smiled at that, and a gleam shone from the edge of one silver tooth. "I want to be mythified."

"I have a favor to ask," I said.

Vic folded the paper and scratched at his gray whiskers. "As long as it don't involve money or lipstick."

"Not sure what it involves, but probably only a few minutes of reaching back to your homeland." I laid the records on the counter next to him.

"You want me to listen to music?"

"A pal procured these in an old traveler's suitcase. The records are of someone chanting—real eerie stuff. And they don't play right either, like the grooves in the wax are stretched or extended somehow. The records seem to run longer than they should, as if they won't end." I looked at Vic to make sure he didn't think I was cracked. He just nodded, so I continued. "Anyway, I think it's an Eastern European language, Baltic origins or something. Lot of 'V' and 'Z' sounds. We want to know what they're saying in the chants and maybe if there's some value in these. Who better to turn to than my old Hungarian pal in the antiquities market, eh?" I smiled, though maybe a bit too much.

"Sounds curious," he replied. "But I don't have a record player."

I laughed inwardly, wishing Joey was there.

"I'll pass it around to someone else I know," Vic added. "These discs look handmade, so you never know what's recorded on them. Probably nothing more than a family choir recital. Come back in a week—next Friday morning—and I'll let you know what I find out."

"Thanks, Vic."

"Don't think about it." He puffed on his cigar and looked around. "Now buy something, would ya? The store don't run on my favors."

Not feeling any great inspiration, I picked up a couple science fiction paperbacks showing covers of green-skinned aliens and spacecraft that looked like flying dinner plates.

When I got home, I tossed the books into a box with a hundred other paperbacks I would probably never read. Besides clothes and makeup, used books were the most common item I found inside baggage. It seemed nearly everyone carried a book about mystery or adventure or advice when they traveled.

I farted around for the next few days, talked with Gail on the phone each evening, and made plans to accompany her and her boss to dinner on Tuesday at Frantillo's. I always enjoyed chatting with Gail; the day didn't seem properly lived if I didn't cap it off with her spirited conversation.

Anyway, that date at Frantillo's wasn't until midweek, so I should have had plenty of time to prepare. Of course, Tuesday afternoon arrived sooner than expected, and I found myself scrambling at the eleventh hour to make her schedule.

Don't be late, Gail had said. *You're always running behind, so leave early if you have to. Be here at five thirty. It's my boss, Geoff Van Duyn, and his wife. Don't make me look bad.*

Her words rang in my head when I ran into Joey in the lobby of Les Deux Oies. I had just bought a bouquet of calla lilies for Gail from the corner vendor and was rushing back to my room to change into dinner clothes.

Joey came out of the elevator when I was about to go up. He looked peculiar somehow, messy in a way that was antithesis to his customary care in grooming: polished shoes, oiled hair, shirts pressed so tight that finding a wrinkle was like searching for fins on a pigeon. Now he was pale, and I guessed he hadn't shaved since last I saw him.

"Joey," I said. "You okay? You look terrible."

"Sorry, Charlie. I didn't know I had to impress anyone today."

"Fair enough. Suppose I did put my foot in my mouth."

"Don't worry about it." He paused, holding the elevator open for me. "Going up, or am I holding the doors 'cause I got nothing else to do?"

Sometimes when Joey spoke, I couldn't tell if he was wisecracking or in a pissy mood. I got the feeling today was the latter case.

"I've got a few minutes. Why don't I walk with you?"

"Suit yourself." He let the doors close and we passed through the lobby.

"Find anything new on those records?" I asked.

He seemed to flinch slightly and walked a step faster.

"I've been listening to them every day," he finally said. "But I still don't know what any of it means. They're all the same, by the way. Every record is the same, 'cept I've noticed one thing."

"What's that?"

We reached the glass doors that led outside to the street, and just before pushing through, he stopped. Joey glanced around as if making sure nobody could overhear him, and his voice lowered.

"After that first voice chants for awhile, a second voice joins in, repeating the words of the first voice. But the second voice is different on each album. Some are a man's and some are a woman's; some sound old and some young. They're a different person joining in, but, otherwise, the records are the same. That god-awful music and the creepy chant. *Vkhodite. Vkhodite. Vkhodite.* I never heard of such a thing."

"Do you..." I started to say, then stuttered, not sure how to phrase the question. "When it's playing, do you still feel the same, like what happened in my apartment?"

He nodded, and his voice lowered even more.

"It's strange, Charlie. Even when I'm not listening to a record, the music keeps playing in my head. It's like it won't turn off. But I don't want it to turn off, either. It makes me feel good, like it's *supposed* to be playing, like it's sharing a great secret."

"Maybe you shouldn't play it for awhile. As you said before, it could be some sort of hypnosis. Who knows what's it's doing—could be rewriting your brain. Turn it off until we figure out what it is."

"But that's just it," he said. "I think the records are telling me something. They *want* me to know. I'm not saying the music is swingin' good times—it's a pretty wretched sound—but it changes as you listen. It causes you to visualize things. I see a clearing in a forest that's covered in snow. I see a faraway castle with turrets that look like Christmas tree ornaments. The records are preparing me...a new life, away from pain and fear."

Joey's eyes seemed to glaze over.

"That sounds pretty cracked to me," I said.

Maybe I shouldn't have been so blunt in my response. He startled, and a dark shadow passed over his face. I wondered later if I would have nodded understanding and inquired further, Joey might have opened up a bit more. He might have told me *whom* he saw in his visions, what he expected, and what was told to him.

Instead, he clammed up. "Yeah, you're right. It's crazy talk. I've got to go anyway. You're not going to follow me around all day are you?"

"I've got my own plans."

"Good seeing you, Charlie."

"We still on for Roman's auction this Thursday?" I asked, as Joey pushed through the doors to exit.

"Wouldn't miss it," he replied and was gone in a blink.

My side venture with Joey took no more than fifteen minutes. But by the time I went up to my room, dressed for dinner, searched for my car keys (somehow fallen behind the wood locker of a ventriloquist dummy), returned back downstairs, and drove across the city to meet Gail, I was mortified to see that time had skipped forward in a hurry. My watch read five forty-five.

The parking lot at Frantillo's was filled, so I went around the corner to find a space for my car. I fast-walked back to the restaurant feeling every second ticking away in my head. Frantillo's was a small joint, low-roofed and snazzy with big windows covered by thick crimson blinds. The afternoon sun still hung high, and it played funny tricks in the reflections of the glass. I imagined Gail looking out at me from behind the curtains in disappointment.

Inside, the maître d' barely looked up before asking if I had a reservation. I'm sure he thought I was riffraff. He smelled of cheap aftershave and French cheese.

"I'm expected," I said. I walked past, and he shook his head as if I were lying.

The bar area was packed with young businessmen decked out in wide-lapel suits and shoes so shiny it was like walking past a row of mirrors. Everyone in there could have been part of a collection of animatrons; they looked the same, laughed the same, talked about the same topics. *Business meetings, business clients, business opportunities.* It was a world I despised.

Maybe I loathed it because I had once tried to fit in, only to flounder helplessly instead. Failure rears resentment.

I don't know why I let it bother me; I was as happy with life as I deserved and should only wish the same for everyone else. I passed into the dining room, which was arranged in a maze of high-backed booths allowing privacy to each party from surrounding patrons. The lighting was dim, and Italian ballads drifted over muted conversations. I zigzagged through until I found Gail. She sat by herself at a table with three half-drunk glasses of red wine.

"Hi." I waved. "Sorry I'm late, dear. Only by fifteen minutes this time."

"Try twenty." She got up to meet me, wearing a tight shirtwaist dress with big black buttons that looked ready to pop off. Though she was a few years older than me, Gail could doll herself up to look half her age. She was a full-sized woman with curves like a pair of necking swans.

"Twenty's not so bad." I leaned in for a smooch.

She pulled away. "Twenty today, thirty yesterday, an hour tomorrow. When are you going to win a working clock at one of your auctions?"

"Brought you something," I said and handed her the calla lilies I'd been carrying since the apartments. "Won't you feel bad for scolding when I explain how I scoured the florists of Detroit, handpicking only the finest of lilies for your pleasure?"

"I might if it were the truth," she said.

Gail accepted the flowers, and my charm won over her scowl. She smiled, and we kissed.

"Did I miss much?" I asked.

"Geoff's mingling at the bar. He saw some buddies from a club—either polo or yachting or men of inherited fortune—and went over to show off his wife. She's nineteen years younger than him, you know. Took their second honeymoon last month."

I rolled my eyes. "I sure fit in."

"You can try to make me look good. He's heading up store expansion in the New England markets and I'm in the running for a promotion. A woman with a man does better climbing the corporate ladder than a woman without. You know how much trouble we can get into if left to our own devices." She pinched the inside of my thigh and winked.

I startled, and a tiny squeal slipped out. "You jezebel!" I pinched her back.

She never pressured me, but I knew a married woman did better yet than any unmarried one, regardless if she was in a relationship. Gail wore a small diamond ring on her wedding finger that I gave her some years back. It wasn't an engagement ring or even a promise ring, just something I won inside a satchel at a baggage auction and gifted her to make up after an argument. But it served a purpose also, as long as nobody asked too many in-depth questions.

"So how are you?" she asked. "Busy day in the junk trade?"

"I made a few dollars."

"Enough to take me to dinner next week? Just you and me, maybe a night of dancing at Morton's Jazz Club?"

"I think that could be arranged."

She ran a finger along the back of my hand. "We don't get out enough, Charlie. It's always nice just to be with you."

"Agreed," I said. "Maybe we can get together this weekend."

Gail nodded as Geoff Van Duyn and his wife returned to the table.

I sighed inwardly. Van Duyn looked as if every businessman I had passed at the bar were rolled up into one mega-agency man. Though I'd never met him, I knew much about Van Duyn through conversations with Gail in which she'd recite each workday's highs and lows, her projects and aspirations and office gossip. I knew he liked theater but not sporting events, yachts but not planes, stocks but not bonds.

Van Duyn liked his coffee black, his ties red, and his wives blonde.

Gail worked in the corporate office for Rockwell's department stores, a chain of high-end retailers that carried everything a modern family could want, from clothes to bedding to appliances to toys. She managed procurement for designer women's clothes, some of it pretty hoity-toity fashion. I needled her whenever I won a piece of luggage with Rockwell's dresses tucked inside; everything became "second-hand" eventually. I purchased things for pennies of what she sold on the racks.

Van Duyn was Vice President of purchasing. He was her boss and, as such, determined her future with the company.

Introductions were made, and he started right in on me.

"You a businessman, Charlie?"

"I'm self-employed."

"No kidding. A self-made man?"

"A man still in the making," I said.

He guffawed like a cat choking up a hairball. "Funny stuff." He turned to Gail. "You didn't tell me he had a sense of humor."

"That's Charlie," she said, and I could sense the nervousness in her voice.

"So what is it you do?" Van Duyn asked.

"I'm involved in a few different ventures. I write editorials and buy and sell collectibles."

"Sounds like hobbies, not an occupation."

"I control my own destiny," I said, cringing at the slip of cliché.

"I'll give you that," he replied. "But why knock yourself out, scrambling for pennies? Get a real job, I say, so you have security and can share life's luxuries with Gail."

"Let me tell you, Geoff," I said. "A man is successful if he lives every day with the ability to do what he wants."

Van Duyn nodded, expecting me to continue. I didn't have any more to say on the subject, but they were all looking at me and the silence grew awkward fast. I grasped for something else to add that would seem important.

"Our time on Earth is limited, and there's no point wasting it living someone else's life. Every man's vision of triumph is different, and the truest measure is how honest you are with yourself. Pursue your passion, and success will follow."

What I said sounded so sincere and knowledgeable I wished I'd written it down for future use, though I didn't think I could repeat it again with a straight face. It was probably just recollection of some jumbled phrases from old management pep-talks, back when I *was* in business. But the others nodded and agreed, commenting on the wisdom I'd shared. Van Duyn said if I ever wanted to try my hand in the department store business, he'd have a job for me. A waiter arrived to take our order, and afterwards the conversation changed to lighter topics.

I can't say the rest of the evening was pleasant, but it was more bearable than I'd expected.

Chapter 3

The next couple days passed as if they didn't exist. I felt antsy like there was something I was supposed to do, or else I was missing an affair, the way a celebration occurs and you show up at two in the morning after it's ended. By the time you arrive, everyone is passed-out drunk, the music's turned off, and the pink streamers hanging off light fixtures just look limp and spent. During that time I penned some editorials and nursed a steady, dull ache in my head, sold some collectible spoons to a silver dealer, and wrote a monthly letter to my folks back home. Each night I dreamt of people sitting around a campfire in the snow, like a powwow. Around them spread a forest, and I wondered if it was the same snowy forest that Joey said he dreamt of. The people sitting around the campfire had empty faces, just the shell of an egg sitting on top of a torso, and they disappeared into the night one-by-one.

By the time Thursday afternoon arrived, I was bored and desperate for some action. I'd been waiting for today's baggage auction for a long time; I hadn't been to an auction or race in a week, as all the tracks were closed for the summer heat and most other "venues of chance" were on hiatus. I ironed my pants and dialed Joey at the same time, holding the handset in the crook of my neck while steam drifted up my face.

He picked up after nine rings.

"Hey, it's me, Charlie. You ready? Roman's is opening in half an hour. Want me to meet at your room?"

"Charlie...?" His voice drifted, as if my name were a question or a fleeting memory from something long ago.

"Yeah, from upstairs. You drinkin' already?"

There was a pause between us, and in that lack of conversation I heard dim voices in the background, muffled by distant music, but words repeating, chanting.

The records.

"Hey, pal," he said slowly. "I'm not feeling up to snuff today. Why don't you go on without me."

"Geez, they're liquidating baggage from the Lincolnwood Hyatt today. The Lincolnwood! Kim Novak roosted there last month, vacationing from Hollywood. I heard the porter lost one of her satchels. Who knows what might turn up today."

"Make a bid for me. I'm gonna take it easy."

"You want me to pick up some soup for you on the way back?"

"No, no, pal, it's okay. I'm just gonna sleep it off."

I shrugged, as if he could see me through the phone line. "Okay, hope you feel better tomorrow."

"Thanks," he replied. "We'll be fine."

"Who's 'we'?" I asked, but the line went dead as he hung up.

I never knew Joey to call off plans due to sickness. Catching the sniffles wasn't reason enough to skip playing the auctions. Of course, age *was* catching up to us, and the weather extremes didn't help. As of late, I also had felt sluggish, my mind a bit muddled. Maybe there was a bug going around the hotel. Now that I thought about it, that wouldn't surprise me at all. Who knew what kind of foul things died in the ducts, their carcasses left rotting so the gases of death bubbled out from the hissing vents into our rooms. Les Deux Oies wasn't exactly a sanctuary of sanitation; I'd seen mold in the halls and roaches scurrying into ever-widening cracks. Not a lot, mind you, but their occasional appearances were just enough to remind you that things causing the willies existed all around and there wasn't much you could do about it. I had spoken to the building's superintendent, Horace Wetzel, about the declining condition, but he just nodded and said he'd check it out, all the while giving me that look: *if you don't like it, you can go somewhere else.*

So I did, at least for the evening. I went to Roman's.

By the time I arrived, the auction house was filled with gamblers, investors, goons, and degenerates. It reminded me of a scene from an old James Cagney mobster movie. Groups of men dressed in shiny suits stood around, their eyes hidden in the shadows of low-slung fedoras, and they all turned to me as I walked through the front entrance.

"Charlie, over here," Ray Galler called out. He stood with a couple of bespectacled men who were built skinny and narrow-faced like accountants. "This is John A. and John T." He tilted his head at me. "Johns, this is Charlie Stewart."

"Did you hear Kim Novak's satchel is supposed to be here?" one of the Johns asked.

"Knew since it went missing," I replied with a wink.

"This is the Johns' first time at the auctions. I'm training them to run my stores, and I told them you're one of the smartest bidders to watch," Ray said. He looked past me. "Where's Joey?"

"Took a sick day. Too much sun."

"Huh. Not like him to miss out on something like the Lincolnwood."

"Don't I know it, but what can you do if health deals you a bum hand for the day? Take it and reshuffle tomorrow."

"One less bidder sounds fine by me," the other John said.

I was going to snap something back, real witty, too, but the auctioneer started in on his spiel.

I had twenty bucks in my pocket and was itching to spend it. The first case went up: a caramel-colored piece of luggage with a saddle belt wrapped around each side. I bid my opening dollar and Ray went to two. The dollars increased until Ray won at six and a half. The next item was a checkered satchel. Ray won that, too. An hour later, I still had twenty bucks in my pocket.

I'd been outbid on everything, most noticeably by Ray and the accountants. They must have bought at least three-quarters of the luggage so far.

"What gives?" I whispered to him. "You've spent half the economy of Detroit. You know something I don't?"

"Feeling lucky today, Charlie. It's more than Kim Novak who's stayed at the Lincolnwood lately."

That did it. I'd been moping around all week, and I refused to go home empty-handed now. The next item the auctioneer called out was a leather suitcase, its face more cracked than a smiling politician. The edges were frayed and the locks shed flecks of rust.

"Opening bid, do I hear an opening bid for this fine gentleman's case?" said the auctioneer.

"One dollar," Ray said.

"One dollar over there, do I hear two?"

"Ten," I called out.

The auctioneer coughed.

I hated myself. I knew it was a bad bid, a *dabbler* move, but the craving to win had hold. Buyer's remorse was nothing compared with the hasty impulse to make an offer on an item, knowing the auction was soon-to-close; I came all the way down here and I *had* to gamble on something.

"Ten dollars, the man with the big wallet. Now ten, going eleven, going eleven once, going eleven twice. Sold! Ten dollars."

"I wouldn't have gone past two," Ray whispered.

"Sometimes it takes a little jolt to get into the action," I said.

"The action's all gone, buddy. There's only one more case left."

A porter carried out a busted suitcase held together by bailing twine.

"Last item," called the auctioneer. "A promising treasure trove, this case is bursting with potential. Do I hear an opening bid?"

Ah, to Hell with it, I thought.

"Ten dollars," I shouted.

I heard the crowd collectively groan.

Later, as we collected our winnings, Ray approached and slapped me on the back.   "Tough bids," he said, snapping his fingers.

"Just like playin' ball. Some games you're a star, and others you wish you never signed up. Maybe Joey was onto something staying home."

"Who knows, you could find the Queen's Diamond hidden inside."

"Not in these dogs." We both knew I'd been a dummy.

"Listen, the reason I'm bringing the Johns into my business is that I want to spend more time hunting for the *real finds*, peoples' heirlooms and found artifacts. The baggage auctions are great, but I'm fixing on attending antique show circuits and estate sales, connecting with property liquidators and dealers."

"Branching out? There's no one better finding value in the throwaway trade."

"It's all part of a grand plan," he said. The two accountants appeared on either side of him like a pair of guard dogs. "Acquisitions are the key."

The crowd was thinning, bidders making their way to cars waiting outside. Most of the auction attendees were suspicious of everyone else and guarded their wins the way misers watch pennies. I always thought it was guilt that gnawed at men like that; those who stole before were most likely now to distrust the world around them.

I turned back to Ray with the mountain of cases piled around him. He must have bought at least fifty items. "So what do you want? A hand carrying out your winnings?"

He snorted. He snapped his fingers. "I want to see your apartment, Charlie. You and Joey bring some top finds to me. What do you do with the rest of your winnings, the loafers and perfumes and broken toys that most of us cart home like we're the city garbage men?" He toed my case, the one held together by twine.

"It keeps me company at night," I said.

Ray snorted again. Snapped again. "I've been trading collectibles a lot longer than you. Let me take a look at what else you've got. I may find some things in your home with value you don't know about. I could take 'em off your hands."

He was offering to cart out some of my junk *and* pay me? I asked, "Tomorrow afternoon soon enough?"

"I'll be there at three."

I wished him luck for the rest of the night and went out the door.

The trip back to Les Deux Oies was slow-going. I had a Ford and I babied her. She was a powder-blue Crestline, '52 model, lot of miles and a lot of good memories. But she was ailing now, the transmission gears starting to slip and alignment pulling to the right. I'd just replaced a cracked windshield and blown muffler, and I knew some expensive repairs were in my future. I cussed myself out that I'd gotten caught up in the bids and blew through a twenty for no good reason.

Back in the apartments, a funny thing happened. I was going up the rickety elevator, suitcases in hand, along with a man I recognized as one of Joey's neighbors, Martin something-or-other. I didn't particularly know him, though we'd been introduced in passing a year or two ago. He was young and blond, some sort of Scandinavian stock, and married to a gorgeous dame who could have passed for his sister.

"Evening," I said and nodded a greeting at him.

He returned the sentiment.

As we arrived at the fourth floor, I felt a tug in my mind, like a cartoon-hand aroma tickling my senses, enticing me to get off and follow its lead. The doors parted, and Martin stepped out, muttering, "*Vkhodite.*"

"Excuse me?"

He didn't respond, just hurried away, vanishing behind the closing doors. The elevator rose, and the cartoon-hand aroma sensation passed, but I felt the aftereffect; that tingling when you know you've narrowly missed something bad, the out-of-control car coming right at you, and—just when you brace yourself to be hit—it corrects itself and drives away. I sensed it was Joey's room calling me, and my gut instinct said to stay away. My gut instinct said to never go down there again.

By the time I settled in for the evening, I'd tossed back two Stroh's beers and set a third on top of a hope chest that once belonged to a woman whose son helped build the Empire State Building. I knew, because inside were photo albums of him wearing suspenders and a flat cap in all manner of poses along the timeline of its construction. I thought often of the photos I possessed of other people's lives, people I didn't know but whose memories I kept stashed under trunk lids. Were these people all dead now? Did they have families who wondered whatever happened to pictures and mementoes passed down from generation to generation until, one day, such remembrances simply absconded into the unknown?

The cases I won were left open on the floor where I'd dumped their contents. I'd spent twenty bucks and lugged home a pair of four-foot paperweights, for all the worth they held. The first case with the cracked face was stuffed with wrinkled children's clothes, and the busted second case contained paperwork relating to a dairy business proposal. I did find one item of interest, hidden under a false bottom beneath the kids' clothes: a nudie magazine from 1939. I thumbed through it and mused that these were simply more photographs of other people's lives come into my possession.

As the deep-sea shadows of night rolled in, I found myself contemplative again of life, and the "what if" questions flicked through my thoughts. *What if* I had stayed with my family out in the Kentucky wheatlands, where the sun shone across a wide blue sky like molten gold. Maybe I'd be a hayseed farmer, plowing Poppa's fields and spending afternoons fishing in the Blueway River with little care in the world. *What if* I forgave Danielle, the woman I was engaged to a decade ago, who cheated on me with the jockey? Maybe we'd be settled now with a couple of children, living in a cottage down by the lakeshore. *What if* I never met Danielle? Maybe I'd be more open with Gail, more trusting to share my feelings with her...I'm sure I would have proposed by now. *What if* I had managed to keep a "real" profession, accounting or insurance, something stable where I could surrender to those long hours but feel the elusive hope of "security"? I thought I'd be dead from a heart attack. *What if*

Momma and Poppa were right? Nothing good ever comes from moving to the city. What if, what if, what if...

The world turned off, a television show that cuts away to a black screen. Maybe the channels turned, for I was taken to slumber, and, in dreams, saw again the faceless people in the winter forest. There were perhaps forty or fifty men and women settled around an enormous campfire. I felt alone, cold and adrift, and I wanted to join them. At that thought, a blurry figure rose from their assemblage, arms open in welcome. He possessed no real form, no features, just a sense of flowing robes and ethereal limbs. Through him, *inside him,* I saw the universe twinkling like the floating embers.

Come in, he said. *Come in from the cold.*

And I wanted to join them, that group settled in trance around the flames. But I knew, too, I would give up something if I did, something I held dear, some part of myself. I fought the urge to move closer.

The figure's voice became angry.

Come in, or I will take you...

Chapter 4

The next morning was Friday. I brushed aside remnants of the strange dream and made chicken soup and fried some eggs for breakfast. I cooked an extra portion and brought it down to Joey's apartment.

I heard the record playing halfway down the hall before I reached his room. The walls were thin as a weekday newspaper, and I wondered that his neighbors didn't complain. How long had the chanting songs been going on for? All night, or did he wake up and start playing them when he rolled out of bed? I wondered, too, how far echoes of that music could drift.

"Hey, Joey," I called out and knocked on his door.

No answer. I pounded several times until a woman across the hall opened her door. She had blue hair from a bad dye job, wrapped in pink curlers to make it look even worse.

"You playin' a conga over there?" she said.

"Sorry," I muttered.

I had a key to Joey's place, but I knew not to use it unless it was prearranged or an emergency. We both kept keys to each others' apartments in cases of turning off the gas or bringing in the mail if one of us was away for awhile. I didn't think today would constitute an emergency, but I knew, too, that he'd been real sick.

I let myself into Joey's room and closed the door behind.

His apartment looked as if an earthquake had struck, knocking all his belongings down, and then cleaned up by a tornado, tossing them into great heaps. There were luggage and collectibles filling the room, mirroring my own apartment, but thrown in teetering piles against the walls rather than stacked and organized. Normally he was like me, a sucker for collecting, but also tidy, keeping the place in a livable condition. It seemed now that he'd just shoved everything aside in order to have one large, empty area in the middle of the living room.

That's where I found him, listening to the record player, sitting on the floor in a sort of trance, and chanting along with the strange musical words.

Vkhodite. Vkhodite. Vkhodite.

Ne zaderzhivat'sya v kholodnyy i temnyy, ho prisoyedinit'sya ko mne v svet navsegda.

"You alive in here? Didn't you hear me knocking?"

No response. He kept chanting, and I noticed his body swayed just slightly, rocking back and forth.

I stepped closer to him. "Joey!"

At the same time, he stopped chanting and turned to me, and I saw a flash of movement in my peripheral vision. I tried to look in two separate directions: in one, I saw Joey looking sicker than ever, his eyes milky and skin pale-blue, and in the other direction the after-image of a figure that vanished, a wild-bearded man in flowing robes. I tried to exclaim at both simultaneously.

"God, Joey, are you okay?" and "Who else is in here?"

I was so taken aback, though, my words mixed and came out instead as an incomprehensible babble: "*God—who—Joey—else—you—in here!*"

"Charlie, you all right?" he asked.

"Who's asking? The guy that looks like he's been drowned for three days? I've never seen someone pale as a dead fish before."

"I look like that?"

"Yeah, pretty much." Then I rephrased the *other* first question I had tried to ask. "Who else is here?"

"No one but us chickens."

"There was a man, with crazy hair and a beard, like he hadn't shaved in a century."

Joey's mouth fell open, and I could see, even from a distance, he hadn't brushed his teeth in a long time. "You saw him?"

"So there *is* someone?"

"I don't know. I was dreaming of snow and sky…the bearded man was leading me through, so I wouldn't get lost."

"Don't get nutty." I turned and called across the apartment toward the bed and bathroom. "Hello? Come on out."

"No, Charlie, he ain't here. You just saw my dream, is all."

The record was still playing, that cacophony of crashing instruments and solemn words repeating its strange invocation. I felt dizzy, yet ethereal at the same time, like if I fell I would slip *up* an inverted slope, lifted by a reversal of gravity.

"Turn that crap off!" I yelled. Even when I said those words, though, part of me wanted to settle down on the floor right next to Joey. I sensed a great revelation forming, a secret gift offered if only I would listen to the record. But, more than that, I just felt flustered and confused, the way a dream twists your perception.

Joey moved in slow-motion, still seeming to sway back-and-forth. He tilted his head as if trying to comprehend my request, and I saw the quarrel in his eyes, the internal dispute as part of him demanded to let the music play. Maybe he was worn down, or maybe he obliged for my sake, but Joey hesitantly lifted the needle off the disc.

Still carrying the food I made for him, I walked into each room, looking for the bearded man in robes. Joey's apartment was small, even more so than mine, and the doubt quickly formed in my mind as to having seen someone else at all. The amount of baggage and rubbish in here was piled to the ceiling in heaps of such disarray that looking in any direction created hints of monsters and madness peeking from under skewed cases. An assortment of footlockers rose above my head, stacked in ragged formation the way a brick wall appears after a cannonball has smashed through. Behind me, a pyramid of suitcases and cardboard boxes shifted like a wave. A mound of clothes spilled from an open closet, and a pungent smell leaked from its shadows.

And it was cold. Colder than the room should have been, colder than it *could* have been. Air conditioning was not a luxury afforded dependably at the Les Deux Oies. We sweated in our rooms most summer days, finding respite through box fans with damp clothes hung over them, listing strategically in each corner. But the fans did not blow today, and yet it was chilly as January's shore on Lake Erie.

I returned to the living room, and Joey still sat on the floor, knees pulled up to his gaunt chin.

"I told you he ain't here," Joey said.

"Do me a favor and don't listen to those records anymore," I said. Joey nodded, and his eyes looked in my direction, but they seemed to look *through* me, rather than at me. "I mean it, give it a break."

"Sure thing," he said. "I need a rest, anyway."

"I made you some eggs and soup. Where should I put it?"

"Anywhere, Charlie. I'm not that hungry."

"You need to eat. You look like you've lost thirty pounds over the week. In fact, you look like you need to go to the hospital."

If Joey had appeared wan and disheveled when I saw him in the hotel lobby on Tuesday, he was a soup sandwich now. His week's worth of whiskers were salt-and-pepper bristles that looked splotchy as charred embers. His hair was dull and matted and hung over his ears. He still wore the same powder-blue button-down shirt from when I saw him last, and it looked now as if it could stand on its own. But it was his skin that was the worst. It looked watery—translucent—like if I examined close enough I could see his bones and guts underneath. It's how I expected a man who was starving to death to look after a couple months, not just a few days.

"No hospital, Charlie. I just need some rest," he said. "I haven't been sleeping so well lately. The bearded man follows me in my dreams. He wants me to listen...he's trying to save me."

"The more you talk, the worse you sound."

He shook his head at an odd angle, the way someone does after swimming and trying to get water out of their ears. "Sorry, pal, I'm all right. Just this cold, you know? Makes me say funny things."

"Speaking of cold, it's freezing in here. How'd you get the superintendent to install working air conditioning?"

"Wetzel? He wouldn't do me any favors. He's been up here twice complaining the music's too loud."

"At least I'm not the only one who thinks those records are bad news."

"I don't know what it's all about, Charlie. I just have this compulsion—a *craving*—to keep listening. Even when I think I've turned it off, it's still playing."

I, too, felt the pull of the music, and how long had I listened to it total? Including when I walked in, maybe ten minutes, tops. How did Joey feel, who spent every day of last week locked in here alongside the gramophone and discs? I could only imagine the influence it held over him, an influence that seemed to become *stronger*, while he somehow grew sicker.

"Joey, I've never said this before. Nobody loves collecting cases like me, but this record player, this *thing*, maybe you need to get rid of it."

"Not yet. I'll take a rest, but I need to figure it out. It's like shootin' craps; you can't be sure, but just know your number's coming up soon. I feel like that, there's something big about to happen, and I don't want to miss it. I'm so close, Charlie...ready to make a great leap...I know it."

"Well, wait on it awhile. My friend, the Hungarian who runs a book store, told me to return this morning. He was going to research into what these records are saying."

Joey brightened at that. "I'd love to hear all about it."

"Why don't you come with me? Fresh air would do you good."

"No, like I said, I need to rest. That'll sort me out."

"Okay, sleep it off. I'll come back later and check on you. I mean it about maybe needing the hospital, though. You look bad."

"Thanks for the concern. I appreciate it, although you're starting to sound a bit like my mother." He grinned, and it looked almost as if his face split, the lines of his smile dissecting colorless cheeks like tearing across wet paper.

"And don't listen to those records," I added.

"Okay, Ma. Are you going to dress me and send me to Sunday School, too?"

I shook my head slow. "That's some sauce coming from a guy who says records are speaking to him."

Joey laughed at that, a great bellow that warmed the cold apartment. His head tilted back, and a hint of color returned to his milky eyes, and everything seemed as it should. The old Joey Third was back and in control. That's how I choose to remember him, laughing away the sickness, the dreams, the haunted records, laughing like he won the richest bag at the auction.

Though I saw Joey once more, I never heard him laugh again.

Chapter 5

I returned to Vic's Books, driving parallel to the Detroit River most of the way. The blue-green water sparkled and lapped against the piers of Ambassador Bridge. It was a nice drive, which I should have found peaceful, but instead I traveled wrapped in melancholy thoughts. I arrived at the shop and entered as before, the small bell over the door announcing my presence. It was only a week since last I visited, but already the store seemed staler than before, mustier, as if the books were rotting dead things on the shelves of a crumbling mausoleum.

Strange, I thought, *how your surroundings are interpreted to reflect your mood.* When I entered last week, the store felt comfortable, reminding me of happy childhood memories, escaping from the world through imaginary portals created by the likes of Robert Louis Stevenson or H. Rider Haggard. Now the shop felt only dreary and old, a reminder of things that age and are shelved in obscurity.

I moved between the aisles of tomes and found Vic as before, sitting behind the counter and reading, a smoldering cigar stub planted between hardened lips.

"Charlie," he said, placing a marker between the pages of his book. "Right on schedule."

"If nothing else, I am a timely man." I spoke in full confidence but knew that if Gail were there, she'd laugh in my face.

"Timely *and* intriguing," Vic replied. He brought up the pillowcase of records and set them on the counter.

I was going to ask what he meant, but Vic just waggled an accusatory finger at my chest. He exhaled a ring of blue-gray fumes then stubbed out the cigar in a ceramic dish. "I got a friend to listen to your records. The language is Russian... mostly. My friend wants to know what kind of a gag this is, though."

I shook my head. "No gag, unless it was pulled off by whoever made the records."

"No backwards words or dubbed voices?"

I shook my head again.

"Subliminal messages like that Elvis-kid plays in his music to make all the girls turn goo-goo for him?"

His questions began to irk me, as if this were a setup and the real gag was being played on me. "Not that I know of, Vic. If I knew what the records were saying, I wouldn't have bothered you in the first place."

"My friend's name is Yefim László. He works with the Eastern Orthodox antiquities market. He says these are records of the dead."

"Records of the dead?" I repeated. "What does that mean?"

"There are sacred hymns that are chanted and, if performed correctly, lead one's soul to remain intact in another realm after the body fails. It's a sort of spiritual transcendence, or a method of immortality." Vic paused and steepled his fingers under his chin. "The interesting thing about this legend is that it dates back to the Indus Valley People of ancient Pakistan. You ever heard of them?"

"No..."

"They were a civilization of about twenty million people that vanished a few thousand years ago."

"How could twenty million people vanish?"

"That's the mystery ain't it?"

I clenched my teeth. Vic could be a little infuriating sometimes.

He continued. "Of course, that was way before there were devices to record sound. You know the expression that photography is a means of immortality?"

"Sure, it's a way to be remembered forever."

"Consider the philosophy of that statement. At its core, the idea holds true for any medium that records an image or a thought: paintings on cave walls, sculptures from stone, ink on papyrus. Those were visual recordings. Then Thomas Edison came along and invented the record player. The legend moved forward along with the advancement of technology. The hymns could be recorded, so their incantation—their essence—lasts forever."

Goosebumps prickled the flesh on my arms as I thought back, listening to the words spoken by people that were long-dead yet still hanging around. "Why did your friend think this was a gag?"

"He's from Moscow and has a passing familiarity with most of the Baltic languages. The dialect of Russian spoken on these records is old, but there are other languages, voices, he's never heard. Yefim described them as speech patterns like ancient Latin but spoken backwards and guttural, as if recited through a mouth filled with mud."

Vic looked at me, reading for an expression. I didn't know what to say so forced out something, feeling obligated to reciprocate his remarks. "You don't say."

"Charlie," Vic said and leaned in close. "My friend says these records are cursed. They're like reading a demon's diary, they make you sick if you listen. They don't play like normal records. You noticed that already. And Yefim...he says they don't *end*."

I felt my guts sink to my knees. I thought back to when I listened to the albums, how they went on indefinitely, how I tired of listening and turned them off, though I never tried to listen all the way until it stopped. The air in Vic's store felt muggier, *thicker*, and I rubbed at the back of my neck, as if some presence breathed on me from behind. I was about to thank Vic for helping me out, make a quick exiting remark, and then get outside for some fresh air. But he continued.

"One more thing," he said.

"There's more?"

"You want me to quit now, or you want to hear the rest of what's on these records?"

"I'm still here, ain't I?"

"Not long ago there lived a Russian mystic who was said to have learned how to pass between the realms of the living and the dead. Maybe he did it through the hymns of the Indus Valley People or maybe not, but he believed that true salvation came from within, that the spirit of God lived in the heart, not in heaven above. The soul must be *conditioned* for the afterlife, or it would wither into nothingness like a flower, whose roots can't find perch in the soil.

"That man was Grigori Rasputin, the *Mad Monk*. These were his records."

I felt that presence on the back of my neck suddenly burn, like a bull's snort, and I needed to sit. My first thought was that I wanted Vic to keep the records, I didn't want to ever touch them again. But my next thought—the avarice within—wondered as to their value.

Vic seemed to read my mind. "I don't know of any self-respecting establishment that would want these in their possession." He ran his hand over the bundle. "Of course, this *is* Detroit, so not many places here respect themselves *that* much. I could probably put you in contact with a couple collectors of dark artifacts. Maybe get fifty bucks for each disc."

"Sure, thanks, Vic. Like I said before, these don't belong to me. I'm just doing a buddy a favor, asking on his behalf. But I know there ain't much he won't put a price tag on, so I'm sure he'll be interested."

"Yefim said he doesn't ever want to see or hear these records again, and he was pretty insistent I stress that you follow his sentiment. In other words, I'll cross his name off the list of possible buyers." Vic winked at his own joke.

"Thanks again."

"Nothing of it. Your thanks are reflected by your patronage." He extended his arms out to the shelves. "I'm sure you'll find something of interest."

I wasn't much in the reading mood, but I thought I could pick up a gift for Gail, maybe a fiction novel by Valerie Taylor or Faith Baldwin. Gail loved to bury herself in the risqué pulps late at night while we lay in bed. I started to turn away, to skim the shelves for her, when something clicked in my thoughts.

I needed to know more…

"Say, Vic, you got any books on Rasputin?"

Chapter 6

I wanted to tell Joey what I found out and, like I promised, I said I'd return. So an hour later I stood back outside his apartment. It was quiet, and I silently thanked whatever angels were hanging around that he wasn't still playing those damned records. I knocked twice and tried the knob. The door was locked. I could have let myself in again, but I didn't want to seem like a nosy-Nelly, constantly checking on him, walking into his home whenever I felt like it. Anyway, I figured he was probably sleeping.

Another reason I decided to turn tail and get away quick was that I felt its pull again. The turntable was still spinning, still calling to me. It might not have been playing at that moment, but I knew it sure wasn't "off" either, in the sense of regular mechanical devices resting sedentary while not in use. A part of me began jonesing to hear it, a slobbering, sweating part that somehow slid Joey's key up into my hand and lifted it to the lock. I thought that must be how an addict feels, a fiend shootin' heroin into his arm every day who decides to go clean, until someone dangles a needle before his eyes.

A whisper snuck into my ears.

Ne zaderzhivat'sya v kholodnyy i temnyy, ho prisoyedinit'sya ko mne v svet navsegda.

I'm not ashamed to admit that I bolted, just turned and sprinted like Jessie Owns in Berlin. The whisper's allure didn't lessen until I rose in the elevator two floors above.

Back in my apartment I deadbolted the door, then paced between boxes, feeling my heart beat staccato. I went to the largest window and gazed outside for several minutes, letting the oceans of blue sky wash away the jitters. Most of the other tenants had views of identical apartments across the street: faded gray produce shops on the bottom level, stacked on top by floors of living quarters for the low-income populace of the city. Fortunately, my apartment's windows faced an empty lot, a barren space in the commercial quarters like the missing tooth from a child's mouth. I had as nice a view as I could hope for and, unobstructed, my place was kept well-lit. The early afternoon sun poured in, splashing the living room in soft hues the color of melted butter, and I began to feel better. I pushed aside a kit of build-your-own globes, set the pillowcase and records down on the kitchen table, and settled into my easy chair.

Though I wasn't in the reading mood, I looked at the book I bought from Vic. It was a biography of Rasputin, written by an ex-disciple who only distanced himself from Rasputin's teachings decades after the mystic's death. Quoted text proclaimed: *The shackles of my soul were loosed, the blinders removed...*

The front cover showed a photograph of Rasputin in middle age, raising his hand in the air like the blade of a knife, and his mouth gaped open in a great void as if the camera caught him mid-sentence. His hair and beard were wild, like a billowing, unfolding creature. But it was his eyes that were most disconcerting. Those eyes were bulging wide, so large they looked as if a child had drawn a cartoon over his features. They were round orbs of snow-white, with specks of coal as the pupils, arched upwards toward the heavens. It was a sinister image, and I wondered not at all how he gained his moniker, the *Mad Monk*.

I turned to the first page and began to read.

Grigori Yefimovich Rasputin is one of the strangest and most deviant men in modern history. He is remembered as a Russian holy monk and prophet with numerous proven incidences of healing that mystified the most educated medical minds of his time. He was also labeled a charlatan who manipulated the suffering of others for political and financial gain. Still today, he is regarded as a shadowy and furtive individual said to have been in league with supernatural forces and granted mystic abilities in exchange for dark servitude. The only fact which has been steadfastly proven is that Rasputin possessed some abnormal power over Russia's last ruling Emperor, Nicholas II and his family, and was instrumental in the fall of the tsarist government, which led to the collapse of the Romanov Dynasty in 1917.

Separating fact from superstition and heresy is challenging, as much written documentation relating to Rasputin has inexplicably been destroyed over the years since his death. Even that which I saw and experienced firsthand while under his sway seems difficult to believe and recite all these years later.

Rasputin was born a peasant sometime between 1863 and 1873 in a small village outside Siberia...

I read further. Soft tick-tocks from the clock on my wall punctuated each turned page. I had been familiar with Rasputin's name as a mythical figure footnoted in school studies I once skimmed over as a boy but never read intimately. He had two siblings, both of whom died young due to drowning-related effects (one drowning outright and the other from illness contracted from near-drowning). Rasputin himself nearly drowned, but was saved and thereafter began to portray indications of supernatural powers.

A court record found in the crumbling vault of Verkhoturye Monastery states that while Rasputin was aged "near-to-manhood," his father, Efim, had his horse stolen. It was claimed that Rasputin was able to envision the theft through a "sense known only to him," and lead armed men to a remote farm where the horse was found and the thief apprehended.

When eighteen, Rasputin was reportedly visited by the Virgin Mary and urged to join the Khlysty sect, an outlawed religious group that practiced exaltation through sexual ecstasy. He practiced his beliefs, "converting" the peasant women of each village he passed through. Indeed, his surname, "Rasputin," soon became synonymous in Russian as "the debauched one"...

An image worked itself into my mind of Rasputin as a conman, preying on the lonely borough wives whose husbands were conscripted to labor or military service. Like hoods I knew in the shadows of Detroit, those granted the cunning and discipline to evade scruples found life to be a flea market, buying peoples' trust with words flimsy as a three-dollar bill. Religion and sex go hand-in-hand, after all, each just manners to escape the difficulties of everyday life, to find meaning in a troubled existence.

I read on, absorbing the details of his life, trying to understand the motivation behind stories of his exploits, his wanderings and dark lusts. I searched for a common theme stitching together his philosophies, failures, allies, and enemies; the cults he formed, the followers acquired through practices no other human could replicate.

Rasputin's rise to royal influence came about through his healing of Tsar Nicholas II's only son, young Aleksei, who was dying from hemophilia, a medical condition that impairs the body's ability to stop bleeding. From that time forward, Rasputin was deemed a "holy man" and a friend of the ruling family. His influence extended amongst the Tsar's wife, children, court nobles, and even bishops in the Orthodox Church.

With his political fortitude established, Rasputin began to preach openly and without fear of consequence, of reveling in immoral acts and even consorting with spirits. He was found guilty, though never sentenced, of raping a nun. He spoke with the dead, prophesized the future, and ordered followers to his bidding, which included kidnapping, assault, and even murder. His disciples came to be known as "The Misbegottens," and I shamefacedly admit to naming myself among their number.

During the onset of World War One, in particular, the whispers of Rasputin's dark servitude seemed true. I was alongside him in Rome on June 28, 1914 and heard him speak in tongues never before heard. Yet sailors in the middle of the Caspian Sea swore in court that Rasputin boarded their vessel that very day and flew away on wings of black, carrying off the third mate. On June 28, also, Archduke Franz Ferdinand of Austria was assassinated in Sarajevo. Witnesses testified Rasputin chanted strange words and stood next to the man who shot Ferdinand.

The outside world seemed to fall away while I was engrossed in the book, and I lost track of the time that passed. My imagination filled with Rasputin and the absurd accusations leveled against him. No matter how evil the man's motivations may have been, what was claimed he caused—and was capable of doing—was simply physically and scientifically impossible. I began to disregard the pages I read as mere tabloid fare, similar to the science fiction books I bought from Vic. Just because a book title states it is a biography based on fact does not mean it hasn't been embellished with fine words to attract sales.

I skipped a few chapters, skimming for anything I could relate to...

By 1915, Rasputin claimed to foresee his own impending death. He sought the methodology to remain living even after dying, and became obsessed with the variants of immortality and of finding the means for souls to travel between the worlds of death and of the living. He said: "My hour will soon come. I have no fear but know that the hour will be bitter for you. I will suffer a great martyrdom...and will inherit the kingdom."

During the last months of his life, Rasputin was rarely seen, yet those closest to him vanished without explanation. It was said that he collected souls to fulfill the great prophecy of a vanished people.

I skipped more pages, until some compulsion caused me to flip halfway through and begin reading in earnest.

...When encountered at night, Rasputin was said to chant incessantly. He collected certain "words" according to their etymology, and he filled them with dark power, the way other men might fill a bucket with water. Such words that he spoke had much more meaning than their

surface definition. Words that Rasputin empowered could become an invitation or a password, a remark shared like a secret handshake that, the more spoken, grew only in potency.

Words like, 'Vkhodite.'

My mouth unhinged, and every piece of baggage in my apartment seemed to gasp alongside me.

For Rasputin, 'vkhodite' was the ultimate communiqué of influence. Translating to "come in," the word became the banner command of submission and the proved intention to submit to his discipline. Vkhodite meant to "come into" his world, his dogma. You were surrendering yourself to a higher power, leaving behind the cold and fleeting solitude of earthly existence for immortality under his command. In effect, he was setting himself up as a god and his 'Misbegottens' his disciples.

Rasputin would induct his followers as such: Ne zaderzhivat'sya v kholodnyy i temnyy, ho prisoyedinit'sya ko mne v svet navsegda.

'Do not linger in the cold and dark, but join me in the light forever.'

My God, it was the phrase from the music! Vic's friend *was* right; it really was Rasputin's records.

But if what this author—this former disciple—said was true, how did the chanting on the records hold such an influence over me and over Joey, who was becoming quite obsessed, just by listening to them now, years later? Did those words really hold such power?

I knew then, that regardless of how much of the book was valid, I had to find a way to convince Joey to get rid of the records. The hoodoo-voodoo they spouted carried *some* sort of psychological consequence. I thought about calling Joey and laying it all out, but how could I convince him the few bucks he might turn on those records was worth the effect of a brainwash? I decided I'd go down there tomorrow, take him to breakfast, and lay it all out.

The phone rang, a shrill blast that caused me to leap from the chair like a frightened child. Though it startled me, it was nonetheless a welcome interruption from my dreary thoughts.

I caught my breath and answered. "Hello?"

"Hi." It was Gail, and I relaxed. She was a needed respite from what I just read. She continued. "What're you doing today?"

"Just thinking about you," I lied.

"Good answer."

"Yourself?"

"I'm home from work early and wondering if you'd like to come over for a Friday night date. I'm going to make chicken and artichoke, and there's a bottle of chardonnay that takes two to drink."

I needed to break and take some time to contemplate matters. An evening at Gail's seemed like a shipshape idea. "Sure, honey. Any special occasion?"

"Well..." her voice softened. "I want to talk. You know, about us."

Oh God, I thought. '*The Talk.*' What I first thought as a 'shipshape idea' now sunk like the *Titanic*. Whenever a woman makes plans just to talk, it means she wants something that requires a change of your lifestyle.

I gritted my teeth, but tried to keep my voice upbeat. "I'd like that. What time were you thinking?"

"I know how busy you are," she said. My anxiety slipped into defensiveness, as if that were a barb against me for not having a real job. Just thinking about *The Talk* flipped my emotions topsy-turvy. She continued. "What's a good time for you?"

"I can make time whenever you like," I replied.

"I mean, what time can you commit to? Punctuality isn't one of your finer points, and I don't want to serve dinner cold."

Another barb? I already wished I had said I was too busy to meet. "How about at five? That's two hours from now. I'll start getting ready and maybe even arrive early to show what a changed guy I can be."

"Just on-time is good enough. I can't wait to see you," she said.

"You too. I'm really looking forward to it."

A knock sounded at the front door.

"Someone's at the door," I said. "Gotta go, but I'll see you later."

"Okay, five o'clock. Love you."

"Love you too."

I hung up the phone, first feeling grateful for the interruption, then feeling guilty for feeling grateful. I went to the door.

It was Ray, baring a big smile and a clipboard.

"Hey, Charlie, how's it going?"

"Just living life. What brings you by?"

"We had a hot date, remember? Three o'clock, I'm here to peruse the knickknacks you've been hoarding."

Nuts. I knew I was destined to be late to Gail's. Again.

"Actually, slipped my mind," I said. "I'm not really prepared—"

"Sounds like you need a secretary." He pushed his way inside and whistled. "And a housekeeper."

I had to imagine what my apartment looked like to someone for the first time. Although I knew Ray expected it—the only difference between us being that he owned stores to place his winnings into instead of piling them in his living room—I still felt the scarlet blushes of shame. The walls of luggage I collected looked like the hedges at City Park, cut into an elaborate maze where one could wander lost all day. I don't know how I let it build up so much; it was overwhelming to think of the day I'd ever have to clear it all out.

Inspiration struck. I said, "I'll cut you a deal if you take away everything all at once."

Ray just rolled his eyes. "Funny. Most of this you couldn't give to the homeless."

"So you came all the way over here to insult me?"

He snapped his fingers and slapped my back. "Don't get so tense. I know there's valuables in here I can pay cash for."

"All right. You want to start over there?" I said. I led him to a half-wall separating my dining area from the kitchenette. I had created impromptu shelving out of luggage stacked in different directions and, in the spaces created, stored a deluge of kitschy sculptures, glassware, and tin devices whose purposes were meaningless to me. "I've got some curiosities that came from an Egyptian bagman."

"Egyptian is always a good start."

After half an hour, Ray had ferreted through only a corner of my collections. I started getting antsy, watching the time. I originally thought he might only take a cursory glance, buy a few things, and be off, but he buried himself inside mountains of suitcases that I hadn't looked at in years. He reminded me of an archaeologist, carving through the substrate with a hand spoon, carefully logging every detail in a grid of sectioned quadrants. I wanted to tell him to speed it up, but he was so thorough, setting aside things I forgot—or maybe never knew—I possessed, including jade teacups from China, Mediterranean lithographs, a Royal Air Force jacket, and Art Deco-era dining utensils made of colored glass. Money signs danced before my eyes.

"I gotta make a call," I said.

"It's your place."

I dialed Gail, hoping she hadn't gotten too started on dinner, and fumbled through my mind a number of excuses as to why I would be late. The phone just rang. I let it jangle twenty times, then hung up and called again. Still no answer. I cursed three shades of blue. Tonight wouldn't go well if she had a big talk planned and I blew it off.

I considered Ray a good friend, but not good enough to leave in my home unattended where he could "find" something and take it away without telling me—I simply would never know if anything went missing. But his bright excitement caught me; every few minutes he was muttering *wow* under his breath and setting things aside, and I knew I was earning money just watching him.

On the other hand, no amount of money was worth the guilt of skipping on Gail's dinner.

"Ray," I said. "I hate to interrupt you, but I'm going to have to ask you to wrap it up."

"You kicking me out already, Charlie? I thought we were doing business."

"We are, but we'll have to pick up another time. I'm sorry. It's my fault I overbooked today."

"I came all the way across the city for this."

"Don't chafe. I think you could spend all week in here and still not be done."

"If you let me." His eyes twinkled. "You've got some notable effects stashed in your belongings."

The phone rang, and I prayed it was Gail checking on me, knowing I was running late. Maybe I could salvage this afternoon after all.

"Hold that thought," I told Ray. Into the phone, I answered, "Hello?"

"Charlie, I've got an offer for you."

It was Vic. Normally I'd be happy to hear from him, but now wasn't a good time. Then again, anytime was good to hear an offer.

"I'm listening," I said.

"My friend, Yefim László—the one who listened to your records—wants to buy them."

"I thought he never wanted to see or hear them again."

"That's what he told me, but I guess people are allowed to change their minds. He's here now, and he wants them."

"They're not my records to sell—they're my friend, Joey's. He lives downstairs, and I'll have to arrange a meeting between them for another time."

"Yefim is hot to buy right now."

"It'll have to wait. I'm in the middle of a couple other deals."

Vic's voice lowered, as if he were whispering. "Charlie, I've never seen my friend like this. I tried talking him out of it, but he's prepared to spend a great deal of money to procure those records immediately. He says time is of the essence. Maybe he learned something we don't know, but your friend could be in for a windfall."

My nerves burned. I was about to tell Vic there wasn't a chance in Hades I would set up a meeting right now with Joey as sick as he was and me running so late. But then I thought, *this was an out*. Those records were no good—I knew that in a way that didn't make logical sense—and maybe this was a way to get rid of them. Whoever's hands they ended up in would be away from Les Deux Oies. Somebody else could figure out those hellish chants and dreams of a crazy man.

I hoped Gail would understand...she'd have to.

I spoke into the phone. "I can't guarantee Yefim an audience with my friend, as he's been real sick lately. But he can come over and I'll bring him down for an introduction."

I heard Vic relay my response to Yefim and then his excited reply.

"I'm in the Les Deux Oies building," I said. "On Sanford Street. Sixth floor, apartment number six-twelve."

"Yefim gives his thanks and is on his way."

"All right. Thanks, Vic."

"And, Charlie," he said. "Don't fleece him too badly. I've never seen Yefim like this, so...desperate."

We hung up, and I saw Ray standing nearby, acting inconspicuous, but obviously listening to the whole conversation.

"What was that all about?" he asked innocently.

"People are going to think we're holding a convention in here. Another collector's coming over."

"And this after you tell me I have to leave?"

"I'm bringing him down to Joey's place. He wants to buy some records Joey won last week."

"What kind of records?"

"The kind you don't want," I said.

Ray snapped his fingers once, loud. His face tightened into a scowl. "Charlie, I hope you're not holding out on me. Who buys your wins when nobody else does? I throw myself at you, offering you dough. And here you are giving the inside scoop to another dealer? I think I should get the right to bid, too."

"Ray," I said and paused, not knowing how to explain myself without sounding four cents shy of a nickel. "The records are no good, trust me. They're in another language, and they hurt your ears, they sound so bad."

"Yet someone wants to buy them this very moment."

"I don't know what this guy wants them for, but it's a bad investment."

"Maybe I can judge for myself."

My exasperation was growing out of control. I felt people were walking all over me with what they wanted, and I couldn't put my foot down hard enough to control them. "Fine, but I'm telling you it's a waste of your time."

Ray nodded slightly. "We'll see," he said, and went back to rifling through the suitcases.

I tried calling Gail again, but she still didn't answer. I wondered if it was on purpose—she knew that if she picked up, I'd snake my way into canceling, but if I couldn't get a hold of her, the guilt would drive me to rush over there one way or the other. Which was true. I heard that rich socialites were beginning to use "answering machines," like robotic secretaries, and that someday it would be commonplace for every phone to automatically have the ability to record a message. Did I wish we used that technology today...

I didn't have time remaining to shower and shave like I wanted, but I got cleaned up as best I could in the reduced amount of time. I planned to drop off Yefim and Ray at Joey's and go from there straight to Gail's. I towel-washed my face in the sink, trying not to look too hard at the features of my weathered mug. Gail said the wrinkles around my mouth and the crow's feet at my eyes gave me "movie star character," but I thought they just made me look prematurely old. Not that I cared much about my appearance. I had never been a lady's man in the looks department and, as I aged, I knew it mattered less and less.

I wound my way through stacks of baggage until I reached the closet. I pushed aside uniforms, costumes, and vintage finery until I reached my own clothes, and selected a charcoal gray suit with olive pinstripes. I heard a tumbling thud from the living room, followed by a clattering like loose coins rolling across a tile floor.

"I'm all right," Ray called from the living room. "Some of your cases took a tumble."

I didn't reply. Just dug around until I found some clean dress socks and shoes that weren't dull enough to need a shine. Picked out a silk tie that was soft as clouds. It was one of six dozen found inside a lacquered salesman's trunk I won at an auction last year. That had been a good bid; I'd never have to buy a tie again for the rest of my life.

I knotted it, and someone pounded at the front door. Pushing my way past luggage towers, I returned to the living room, where Ray scoffed. I answered the door, prepared to feel the embarrassment of someone else seeing my place for the first time. The man who answered was old and wiry with the biggest shock of white hair I'd ever seen, overlaying his head like an enormous cotton ball. He was pale, and shook slightly, and barely looked around.

"Mr. Charlie Stewart?" he asked.

"That's me. You must be Yefim."

"Yes. I'm very excited to hear those records again."

"Come in," I said. I motioned at Ray. "That's Ray. Ray, Yefim."

Ray was suddenly all smiles. He snapped his fingers and plunged his hand into Yefim's. "Nice to meet you," he said.

Yefim returned the handshake but barely acknowledged him.

"You listened to the music, yes?" Yefim asked me.

I nodded. "I heard it."

"Has *he* come to you? The man with the beard?"

My chest tightened, as if a vice wrapped around my ribs and pressed in.

"Who's that?" Ray asked. "Another dealer?"

I flashed him the 'not now' look.

"Yes, I think I've glimpsed a bearded man. What does it mean?" I asked.

"Hasn't he told you?" Yefim answered. "Or are you not listening to him?"

"That doesn't exactly answer my question."

"It means there's room for all of us."

My chest tightened more, if that were possible. I thought of the dreams of people grouped around a campfire in the snow. "You've got it worse than Joey."

"He can save you also, if you let him."

"Who are you talking about?" My voice rose. "Who is the man with the beard?"

"It is Rasputin. But I think you knew that already. He's returned as prophesized."

The vice, tighter. There was barely room in my chest to inhale.

"The world is ending soon, Mr. Stewart. Rasputin is here to save us, if you accept him."

"Wow," Ray said and snapped his fingers. "Rasputin?"

Yefim nodded gravely.

"You've got records by the Russian seer, Rasputin?"

"Mr. Stewart's friend has them. He is *the doorway.*"

Ray smiled for all the wrong reasons. "Then what are we doing up here?"

Staying safe, I wanted to respond. But I knew I had to move; it was time to go to Joey's.

"What are you going to do with the records?" I asked Yefim.

"The same as anyone would do. Listen to them."

Suddenly my plan seemed foolish, the strategy of a child who breaks a cookie jar and tries to hide it in the nearest cupboard drawer. I would never be able to contain the mess just by passing it along for someone else to use.

"I hear it playing now," Yefim added. "Below us..."

I thought of the three records that Vic passed to Yefim. Vic had said: *"My friend says these records are cursed. They're like reading a demon's diary; they make you sick if you listen. They don't play like normal records. You noticed that already. And Yefim...he says they don't end."*

I wondered how long Yefim had listened to those records while they were in his possession. Did he play them for hours before realizing they never ended? Was he more *infected* with it than any of us? The music seemed like a germ. Once it contaminated you, you might not feel its effects for some time...but when the germ incubates, it infects the listener and spreads into madness. Yefim must have understood after listening that they were cursed and returned them to Vic, but since then the voices grew in his head, calling to him to listen again.

"Below us..." Yefim repeated. He cocked his head, listening to a song I could not hear. He walked out the door.

What should I do? Stop him by force? The records would still play, and Joey would still listen. I decided my original child's strategy would have to do for now. If Yefim took them, at least that would buy me some time. At least the records would be out of the building and, hopefully, their effect diminished on us.

I followed Yefim down the hall to the elevator, and Ray trailed after us, writing in his clipboard.

"I'll help you get the records," I told Yefim. "But you take them far, far away from here."

He didn't respond, and the elevator doors opened to take us inside.

I heard that cursed music as soon as we reached Joey's floor. I imagined a rider on a horse galloping to me from the distance. Every time I heard the records playing, the rider drew closer and closer, great puffs of dust filling the sky behind. Only that rider wasn't coming to greet me—he was coming to run me down.

Yefim seemed almost to be shaking, like he was overjoyed to hear the music. Ray made a face like someone farted in his ear and told him it was a lullaby.

I had sensed those records were bad news ever since I first listened to them, but now I began to feel genuinely scared. It was harder each time I heard it not to just settle down and let it carry me off to whatever dream world it sang about. I fought the temptation and led the others to Joey's door, thinking: *let Yefim take the records away; please just let him take them all right now.* That was followed by the thought that if Yefim didn't buy every one of the records, I would snatch them with me on the way out. Just grab-and-dash, break them over my knee, and apologize later.

We walked down the hall, and I saw the building's superintendent, Horace Wetzel, standing in a daze outside Joey's apartment. His craggy face hung slack and tilted toward the door as if listening to what occurred on the other side.

"Wetzel, what're you doing?" I asked.

He looked at me confused, the expression of someone waking from a deep slumber.

"I got a complaint," he said. "A complaint...but someone called me...someone I couldn't see..."

"So you settled for eavesdropping?"

His mind seemed to clear a bit, and his face flushed. "I run this building. I can go where I damn well please."

"I don't think nosing around is in your job description—"

"You got a problem, pay your rent on time. Then we'll talk," he interrupted.

He turned about-face and marched up the hall toward the elevators. His head kept twitching to the side, though, as he passed, spasms like the aftershock of a particularly violent sneeze.

I knocked at Joey's door, knowing he wouldn't answer. I turned the knob and the door opened, so I entered, followed by Yefim and Ray.

The first thing I saw was that Joey wasn't alone. There were several other men and women sitting with him in a circle on the floor. The Scandinavian, Martin, sat hunched over, arms extended palms-up, as if offering worship to Joey. Next to him, Martin's wife tilted her face to the ceiling, eyes rolled back. The woman across the hall with blue hair was there, swaying back-and-forth, as were a couple other people who looked familiar, but I didn't know by name.

The man with the beard was there, too...*Rasputin*. This time he did not vanish when I looked upon him.

He stood behind Joey, and a strange effect caused me to rub at my eyes. The room seemed blurry, as if a fine mist hung in the air. I looked again and saw Rasputin was also *within* Joey, like a spirit rising from its mortal body or, perhaps, like a form within a form, like those little Russian nesting dolls, in which a wooden figure is stacked inside another wooden figure.

The chanting was louder than ever before. The record player must have been at full volume and everyone in the room sang with it. That sound was hideous: squealing, crashing, scratching instruments that just played over and over, overlaid by the recorded voices. Yefim pushed past me to kneel with the others and began to repeat the words I now knew so well.

Vkhodite. Vkhodite. Vkhodite.

Ne zaderzhivat'sya v kholodnyy i temnyy, ho prisoyedinit'sya ko mne v svet navsegda.

"Christ almighty, it's cold in here," Ray said softly. Then he gasped. "Is that...snow?"

And then I realized why the room seemed blurry. There was a fine veil of snowflakes floating in the air. The baggage stacked against the walls had thin lines of frost hanging off the edges. On top of the nearest stack lay the empty leather suitcase with ivory handle that Joey had won, the case that had contained the record player. Everything in the room seemed paler than it should have been.

Yefim turned to us. "Come in," he said. A puff of fog exhaled with his breath. "Do not linger in the cold."

He returned to chanting, and I felt shammed. Yefim was never planning on buying the records; he just feigned interest in order to find out where they were. He wanted to hear them again, to join with the others.

"Charlie," Ray said and tugged at my elbow. "What's going on?"

"It's those records."

I looked again at Joey and stepped closer to him. I was wrong in thinking Rasputin was "within" him. It was the other way around; Joey was within Rasputin and fading away. I saw Joey only as if he were an afterimage. Rasputin's eyes glowed like burning coal briquettes, and they shone through the veil of snow. Steam lifted off his shoulders. If we were in a snowy forest, it was Rasputin who would be the campfire that we circled for warmth.

"Joey," I said. "Can you hear me?"

The group chanted louder.

I needed to turn the music off, to set them free. I pushed past Joey's neighbors and reached for the gramophone playing in their midst. Rasputin watched me and made no effort to interfere. I should have been leery when a thin smile crossed his face, but I moved forward in my charge with the adrenaline-fueled fortitude of the sanctimonious.

I took hold of the record player's arm and lifted. It took no more than a second, and it was *easy*. The music stopped and, by proxy, so did the chanters. It was as if the spell were broken immediately, and the room turned dead-silent. I was already imagining squeezing my hands around that bearded lunatic's throat.

Of course there had to be a reason he was known as the 'Mad Monk'; I should have realized he kept some sort of hoodoo up his sleeves in order to skip across time and materialize out of a record player.

The player's brass arm turned fluid in my fingers and moved like a wet snake, lashing out with its needle, slicing the palm of my hand. A bright red line opened across my skin, and I released it with a cry. The arm became solid again and dropped back exactly into the position from where I had lifted it. The music—and the chanting—resumed.

Rasputin now spoke, and licks of flame shot from his mouth. "Come in. Do not linger in the cold."

An icy wind blew over me, and Rasputin's robes billowed with a *poof*. I felt light-headed listening as the chanting continued, but it sounded distant, the volume turned down. The air became fuzzier, and I wrapped my arms across my chest, shivering under the thin pinstriped suit.

Why had I come into the snow dressed like this?

Pine trees bristled thick in all directions, and I knew I would be lost if I tried to make my way amongst them by myself. In the distance, on mountaintops, were fairy-tale castles with pink and turquoise spires. The moonlight caused them to glow. Snowflakes settled on my nose, and I felt myself grow numb. It was an effort of great magnitude to lift my legs and move, though there was nowhere I could go. I stood in a clearing with a campfire at its center. The fire was wrapped in robes and a beard.

Vkhodite.

Rasputin rose into the air and held his hands up parallel to each other, about a foot apart, as if supporting an invisible rod at each end. Between his hands, the universe shifted. I saw flames roll across the cosmos, consuming worlds and stars and gods. The infinitesimality of existence consumed my thoughts, much as the flames consumed eternity. I knew not if this were a reflection of the past, or of things to come, or how I fit in; only that I was as insubstantial in its effect as a shadow is in a lightless cave. If I held poison in my hand, I would have drunk it; had I a gun, I would have put it to my head. The despair was a blanket wrapped over my senses, so that I suffocated in its many folds.

Vkhodite.

Then I knew. He showed me these things so I would join him. He offered an escape, a freedom from suffering, a chance to find new purpose as one of his Misbegottens. I would never again be alone, never shiver in the snow of life. *I would never die.* It was only my soul he would take, a pittance for his gift of immortality, and I would play on and on through him. If only I would stop fighting and chant along to the music…

I woke to Ray slapping my face. He wore a silver pinky ring in the shape of a horseshoe, and the edge of its band cut my cheek.

"Snap out of it," he said and shook me like a ragdoll.

The temperature seemed to jump a hundred degrees. I went from standing in drifts of snow to leaning against Ray in the muggy early evening of Detroit summer.

"I gotta slap you again?" he asked.

Ray seemed blurry at first but soon drifted into focus. I spoke, and heard my voice sounded drugged. "No."

"Thought you went loopy on me."

"What happened?"

He let go of me. We stood on the sidewalk outside Les Deux Oies.

"You were talking to someone," he said. "And then your voice just dropped off. You looked like you were sleepwalking, the way you moved, real sluggish and stiff. You sat on the floor with your friends and mumbled some weird words over and over."

"Didn't you feel it?" I asked.

"Yeah, I felt it. That's why I left. I've been drunk enough to know when my senses are slipping away. I picked you up and carried you out."

"They didn't stop you?"

"The man with the beard said something, and the others looked like they might intervene, but you and I were closest to the door. I was quick and, once out, nobody followed."

"Joey needs help."

"He sure does. I don't know what he's gotten himself into. What were they doing up there? Looked like a group of commies praying to the devil. That's some sick stuff." Ray snapped his fingers.

"We've got to stop them."

"You have a plan? I hope it don't involve the police, 'cause they wouldn't care. As long as it stays in the room, that's a solid case of religious freedom. Maybe McCarthy was right all along. We're being subverted by the *pinkos*. Ever since his censure, the liberals have been running the country."

Vkhodite.

It sounded in my head, from far away, calling to me. Was the voice growing stronger the longer it went on? Or did its reach expand as more people sang along?

"But you saw it," I said. "It's like being brainwashed. And for God's sake, it was snowing in there! Police or not, we have to go back, pull Joey out of the room, the same as you pulled me out. Then the others..."

"I don't think you're in a condition to do much of anything. You look like you died and thawed out."

I felt it too. The hot evening air burned my cold skin. My joints ached, and my brain felt like Willie Mays used it for batting practice. But I persisted. "He's my friend. I just...wasn't prepared."

"And you're still not. You're not thinking. What're you going to do differently the next time you go up there?"

I couldn't think of a thing.

Ray continued. "How long has Joey been up there with those records?"

"He's been gettin' an earful every day for the past week, trying to figure them out."

"So a little while longer's not going to change anything. We've got to take matters into our own hands, Charlie. We need weapons."

"You've got a gun?"

"I was at Normandy. I've got a collection."

"I didn't know you were in the army."

"Came back a goddamned war hero. Lot of good it does you after the headlines change."

I was taken aback—the things you don't know about your friends.

"So, what's your plan?" I asked.

Ray started snapping fast. "Like I said, we need weapons. I have to go to my North Side shop; I've got some things in storage there. John's working all night, taking inventory. I'll bring him back with the guns. We could use another man."

I was going to ask "Which John," but I supposed it didn't matter.

"We'll regroup in the lobby," Ray said. "I would bring you along, but I've only got a two-seater, and John doesn't have a car. I think you need to rest up anyway."

I was torn inside. I couldn't let Joey rot away in his room any longer with that...*thing*. I wanted to get him now, but I felt faint, like I could topple over any moment and not get back up. Then again, was I lying to myself? Did I really want to go back up there to try to save Joey, or was I making up a reason to hear the music again, to let myself give up? I already felt lulled into a state of semi-hypnosis. The mind plays funny tricks sometimes, and I couldn't trust my own reasoning.

"All right," I conceded.

"You want me to help you back up to your room?" he asked.

"No, I need to get away, put some distance between myself and this building for awhile."

"Don't go far."

"I've just got somewhere I have to check in at."

Ray nodded. "We'll do it, Charlie, don't you worry. We'll storm them, just like at Normandy."

"What time?" I asked.

"What time is what?"

"What time should we meet back in the lobby?"

He stared at me, and his head twitched just barely. "Yeah, in the lobby. Um, three hours. Meet you here in the lobby...three hours, at ten o'clock."

I felt a brush of déjà vu, like I was experiencing something again, something that had occurred already. The air seemed a little colder, a little darker. Or possibly it was just the sun beginning to fall.

"Maybe I should follow you," I said, and I knew it was my fear working me over; I didn't want to be alone. I didn't have many lifelines to grasp, and he was the nearest. If something happened to Ray, my odds of beating this situation would slip even worse. "It could be better if we stay together. I'll just drive separate."

"Do you hear that?" he asked.

"Hear what?"

Ray looked at me and blinked. "No, I gotta go. Can't keep watching in the rearview for you. We'll meet back in the lobby."

I noticed he stopped snapping.

"In Normandy," he said. "Normandy..."

"Ray—"

"See you, Charlie." He turned about-face and left.

I was left alone on the sidewalk. The streetlamp across the street turned on, then fizzled and went out. I walked the other way, around to the side of the building where tenants parked, still feeling muddled in the mind. The longer I was in the shadow of the apartments, I realized the honest truth was that I *did* want to go back to Joey's room and surrender to the song. I thought of my vision in Rasputin's world and the difficulty of moving each leg; that was how I felt now, as if I struggled to reach my car through a bank of snow. But if the others in Joey's room had given in, it was only because they hadn't been there from the beginning. They didn't see what it did to us, the way I watched Joey fade away. Maybe they believed this was a grand venture, a chance to discover the meaning of existence, but I didn't buy it. It was the devil's deal and a kick in the ass.

I made it to my car. I opened the door and slid behind the steering wheel. Slipped the key into the ignition and…nothing. The engine gurgled and belched but wouldn't roll over. I turned the key again to the same effect. I knew my transmission had been going out, but this was something different. The starter? Carburetor? Rasputin's effort? All I knew was the Crestline wasn't going anywhere tonight. How the world seems to conspire when desperation nips at your heels…

Vkhodite.

I needed to get away. I sensed Rasputin—that thing— reaching down to me from the fourth floor, his arms extending like wisps of flame. I jumped out of the car and ran back around the building, hoping to see Ray before he drove off. He was nowhere in sight, so I just kept on running, all the way down Sanford Street, past its closed shops and darkened windows and old vagabonds sleeping in the alleyways.

A taxi drove slowly in the other direction eyeing me: a middle-aged man running—now holding the stitch in his side and gasping for breath—down the street, dressed in a flapping suit and shoes in which one sole began to crack off. I waved him over and, fortunately, he didn't think I was too crazed. I gave him directions, and he drove me to Gail's.

It was after eight o'clock by the time I knocked on her front door. Gail's bungalow was an architectural turn-of-the-century wonder, cramming five split-level rooms and a kitchenette into only a thousand square feet of space. It might have been small, but Gail's home was sharp. Each room had its own theme and color palette; she decorated to match with the season's fashions. She even let me keep a room so I'd feel more welcome during visits. Of course, it never felt like "my" room without luggage littering under every step.

Knocking at her door reminded me of Joey; I rapped for half a minute without any response. I had a key to her house the same as

I did for him, but didn't want to let myself inside if she was fuming.

Finally, she answered. I tried not to look too hard at the streaks of mascara dried under her eyes.

"I'm sorry I'm so late," I said. "I'm in some kind of mess."

Her eyes went big and pink lips parted like a blooming rose. "Charlie, what's wrong with you?"

"It's a long story, dear. It's Joey; I don't know what to do."

"No, it's you," she said. "You look sick. You're paler than a ghost."

"I am?"

"Lord, I can almost see through your skin."

The tension of the last several hours caught up to me, and I felt faint, like I would collapse right on her doorstep.

"Come in," she said. "You need to lie down."

She led me to the living room couch, and I sank down so quick, I thought I would fall through the floor.

"I'll get you some water," she said and vanished into the kitchenette.

When I woke, another hour had passed. Gail wrapped a couple blankets over me while I slept.

"You're freezing," she said.

"I'll be all right."

"I just called Dr. Adams, but he's out on another call. A nurse said to bring you into the hospital."

"It's only the snow," I said. "The snow's making me cold."

"What snow?"

I blanched…why had I said that? The snow was a dream…

Vkhodite.

It was a record, playing over and over again. That's why it kept repeating, like an album that got scratched; it played the same phrases in a loop, repeating through the disc's groove without moving forward. That's where I was, trapped inside the record's cycle.

I had to turn it off.

Gail stroked my forehead. The warmth of her touch thawed my chill. "Charlie, you're scaring me. What's going on?"

Had I drifted away again?

I bolstered myself to focus. "I—I'm hearing things...seeing things...that are real."

That didn't make any sense at all. She cocked her head and made a face, waiting for more. I finally spat it out, blunt as a brick. "Do you believe in ghosts?"

"Ghosts?" she repeated, and her eyes narrowed as if she were contemplating some underlying meaning to the question. "You mean like spirits that haunt our homes?"

Gail and I had spoken late into the night on many subjects, but the topics of death and religion were not ones we broached in-depth. I knew she affirmed Protestant leanings, as myself, but hadn't visited a church in decades. Perhaps religion, like death, was for the morbid.

"Yes, a presence after death," I replied.

"I think we have a soul, some sort of residue that transcends elsewhere, but I don't really believe in invisible people that remain, wandering amongst us."

"Gail," I said, and paused before continuing. "There's a ghost in Les Deux Oies. It's hurting people, and I think it's taking them away to another place. It's touched me...it's *inside* me somehow, and it's trying to take me, too."

I thought she would step back and roll her eyes and say how the hoarding in my apartment is truly driving me bonkers. Instead, she kept stroking my forehead and kissed my brow as her fingers passed over.

"What can I do to help?" she asked.

"You believe me?"

"If there's something affecting you, I'll do whatever it takes to make it right."

I don't know why, but I always seemed to judge myself more harshly than Gail judged me. My own conscience constantly thought the worst of myself, and it manifested itself onto her. She was the understanding one between us, the rational and considerate partner in our relationship. Even when I was late to see her or pulled a boneheaded move, I knew she would be inwardly disappointed, but she never made as big a deal of it as I did in my own mind. I got into the habit of thinking ill of people—even her—and then, every time when I braced myself for negativity, she amazed me with sympathy and understanding.

"I—I don't know what to do," I said.

"Tell me what happened."

And so I did. I recited everything from that previous Thursday night at the baggage auction where Joey won the record player. I described the chanting we heard and my conversations with Vic, trying to figure out what the music meant. I told her how I watched Joey grow wan, until I saw him last as nothing more than a shadow within Rasputin. I explained the music's effect on anyone who heard it, even Joey's neighbors who were hapless enough to be within earshot of his room. I spoke of the dreams I had and the impossible changes in his room, as if it transformed into another land.

I told Gail everything and, again, braced myself for her rebuke.

"Why on God's green earth are you still living there, if you think a curse is taking over the building?" she asked. "Just leave."

That wasn't the response I expected, though it seemed an obvious question to be asked.

"I believe it's like an infection," I said after careful thought. "It's a seed planted in my brain, and it won't be dislodged regardless of how far away I travel. I've been fighting it, but he's in my dreams, he's in my head, *whispering*. I've got to turn it off, forever."

Gail made a face like she was going to cry, then it seemed to change to a laugh, before returning to the potential waterworks. "Oh, God, the messes you get into, Charlie."

"This is hardly something you can plan on—"

She interrupted, as if I hadn't spoken. "If only I'd talked to you a couple weeks ago."

I didn't like the sound of that remark...a phrase like that could lead to a whole slew of problematic scenarios.

I asked anyway. "About what?"

"You seem so distracted when we're together, like your mind is somewhere else."

I knew better than to disagree with that.

She continued. "I didn't want to bring it up if it wasn't going to happen, but now it has, and I wish I'd have discussed it with you since the very beginning."

"What, Gail? I'm feeling crazy enough without you dragging up something else."

"Geoff Van Duyn made me a job offer to oversee onsite expansion of a new Rockwell's. I'm moving to New York City."

I was devastated. No, I was *crushed*. All the building fear and distress was a weight so great, it felt as if I crawled on concrete while a giant foot squashed me from above. And now here I sat, literally *dying*, and my girlfriend says she's leaving me. Though I'd always expected it, I wasn't prepared for that stab of pain that suddenly made all the other pain seem as inconsequential as a scratch on the thumbnail.

"I'm sorry," I said, more to myself than to her.

"I want you to come with me," she said.

"Huh?"

"Charlie, I know how happy you are in Detroit. You've got your friends, your collections. But what's your future? You're struggling with something every time I see you. My relocation will be paid for and I'll be making good money, more than I need. It's a chance to start over for both of us...together."

My mind reeled, and I couldn't determine if it was Rasputin's curse knocking me or what Gail just said. "That's so...sudden."

"I know, Charlie. But sometimes when your train comes to station, you've got to be ready on the platform, suitcase in hand."

"Is that why you brought me to dinner with Van Duyn?"

"I wanted you to meet him. The promotion was a possibility, something rumored about that I was in the running for. He made me the offer today. I was planning on telling you over dinner tonight...under better circumstances."

"Congratulations." I wasn't sure of what else to say.

"I should have told you what it entailed earlier," she said. "But it was just a rumor, and I didn't want to get our hopes up, or make it seem like I was some girl suckered by daydreams."

"Gail, your timing—"

"Like I said, I wish I would have discussed this a couple weeks ago, when I first heard about it. Maybe you would have been packing your clothes instead of running around at those auctions. Maybe this *thing* never would have happened."

Though I appreciated her stance, I doubted I would have skipped on an auction even if I *was* in the middle of packing.

"We can talk about it later," I said, though I didn't know how much "later" I had. Cold sweat dripped down my temples like melting frost, and I shivered.

"I know," she said. "I'm sorry I even told you about the job when you've got your own problems. I believe you about this haunting, but it's hard to put into perspective, just something I never imagined anyone would actually get tangled up with. I hoped that moving would wipe the slate clean, all our problems taken care of. But there's always a hitch, isn't there?"

I was in fear for my life, and right now all I felt was guilt for burdening her with my woes. My eyes rolled back, and I sensed as if I was about to pass out again...

"Charlie?" Gail shook me and patted my face.

I *did* pass out.

"How long was I gone?" I asked. I sensed Rasputin's presence, but he wasn't alone. I heard Joey call to me as well: *vkhodite.*

"Just a few minutes. You're sick, Charlie. I want to help you with all this, but you can barely stay awake. You need to go to the hospital. If what you say is true—you're infected with some sort of ghost's touch—there's no telling what hideous illness you've contracted."

"Hospitals won't help. I've got to get back and take care of this now. I'm meeting Ray at the apartments. He's got a plan."

"What's his big plan?"

I certainly didn't want to tell her we were going in there for a *stick-em-up.* "We're going to turn the record player off."

"That's it? You defeat the ghost by turning off the record player? If it's that easy, why don't I go over there and do it for you? You're too sick to do anything but sleep."

"No, Gail. You can't go in there. Hearing the music is what makes you sick."

"Wear ear plugs."

The simplicity of her declaration made me feel like a little kid being told that two pounds of turds don't fit in a one-pound box. It was too simple, too obvious, to do anything *but* make sense. Then again, nothing about those records made sense. Maybe ear plugs wouldn't work—the ghost would slip right on through the rubber. Besides that, I already heard the music in my head even when it wasn't around. But I knew, too, the closer I was in its presence, and the more I listened to Rasputin's chants, the greater effect it had on me. The ear plugs, at least, would have to slow down that effect.

"I knew there was a reason I loved you," I said.

"What's that reason? My common sense? What about my support of your crazy ways, and my compassion and cooking and wit?"

"And extraordinary beauty," I added.

"What don't I do for you, Charlie Stewart?" She pinched the inside of my thigh.

"Stop it, I'm near an invalid!" I cried out with a giggle. The stress and fear and sickness passed for a second, just a brief moment in which the sun popped over the horizon and melted that crushing pressure on my back. Then the sun winked out, and the pressure and fear and everything else crashed back into place.

"I've got to go," I said.

She looked at me and nodded. "I'm glad I got to see you."

"I tried calling earlier."

"I knew it was you. Sorry I didn't answer. I thought if I picked up you would cancel on dinner."

"I was going to."

She smiled, but it was a pitiful, sad look, the expression of foreboding and acceptance that whatever was to happen would probably be for the worst. "I'll get those ear plugs for you. The neighbor's dogs have been keeping me up at night. I guess I won't be sleeping tonight anyway."

Gail went into the other room, and I tried imagining life without her. I couldn't. I knew she was right, that I'd grown dependent on her to keep me sane. She was the one constant in my life, like going to the track and knowing she was the winning bet every single race. Just being in Gail's presence relieved my worries, and the sound of her voice warmed me with joy. If I was to be taken away by Rasputin, like Joey, I had to make sure she didn't follow. I wanted Gail as uninvolved and distant as possible. I hoped she'd have the life she deserved in New York, and I knew it was a long stretch to even consider me being a part of it, given the condition I was in. I know how hokey it sounds but, regardless of what would happen, I just wanted her to be happy.

She returned into the room, and I thought of the dramatic final scenes I'd seen in movies like *Gone With the Wind* and *Casablanca*, those "good-byes" that stain your memories forever with tears. I wanted my good-bye to have meaning.

Instead, I planted my face in my hands. "Can you give me a ride back home?"

Chapter 7

Gail asked a lot of questions as we drove back to the apartments. *How was I feeling? What else did I know about ghosts? What precautions was I going to take? What if something worse happened to me? What if I couldn't turn the record player off?* Her string of inquiries didn't instill a lick of confidence in me, and the closer we got to Les Deux Oies, the less I wanted to chat about it.

Above, the moon posed full. I'd never been particularly superstitious, but I thought that boded poorly. Wasn't the night of the full moon when forces of evil were at their strongest? That was when the beasties and demons came out, those creatures written about in monster books or shown oversized on the big screen. There were thin gray clouds, too, that drifted across the sky, and it made the night even more ominous.

We arrived and pulled around to the side of the building where my Crestline sat, looking sadder than a caged dog. Gail placed her hand on my wrist.

"Be careful," she said. "Are you sure you don't want me to go in there with you or wait for you somewhere close?"

"Absolutely not. I don't want you anywhere near this building."

"I'll be too far away if something happens, if you need me. It's a twenty minute drive from my house to here. A lot can happen in twenty minutes."

"I know, but you'll be safe at your home. Wait by the phone, and I'll call you when it's over. I'll be all right for now; I'll be with Ray."

"Good luck," she said and kissed me quickly on the lips.

"Love you, dear."

"Love you, too."

And then she was gone. I stood alone in the parking lot, unsure if I would ever see her again. Hell, I was unsure if I would see the next hour.

I returned inside Les Deux Oies and walked through the lobby looking for Ray or John. The whole floor was empty, and it was silent, too. Usually there sounded the hiss of turning pipes or the echoes of tenant arguments, but now it was so quiet I could've heard a mouse yawn.

I checked my watch, and what I saw caused me to want to punch myself. It was past eleven p.m. People's lives were in peril, and I still couldn't catch up to the world. Ray said to meet him in the lobby at ten o'clock, and I wound up over an hour late. Would Ray have gone up to Joey's room without me or was he still en route? Could this whole situation already be resolved? No, no...*it* was still up there; I felt it.

I needed to make a call. I could go up to my room, but I didn't want to miss Ray if he came through the lobby. I thought about leaving a note if we passed each other, but I didn't have a pen or paper. Fortunately, a payphone stood outside on the sidewalk.

A minute later I stood under the shifting moonlight, digging in my pockets for a dime. I triumphed in that small endeavor and hoped it to be an omen for the rest of the night. I dialed the rotary for Ray's North Side consignment shop. For every ring, I felt my heart beat twice as fast. Nobody answered, and I hung up before it burst.

Where was Ray? This was not good...I wondered if I should just go back up to Joey's room now, alone. I willed myself to wait a bit longer. I returned to the lobby and sat on one of the worn couches lined in pairs against the foyer. The backrests were punctured with knife slits, and springs broke through the seat cushions. More than once in the past, I'd come across a drunk passed out here.

I tried to think up a plan of attack, but I felt dozy. My mind wandered. I imagined the building back in its glitzy hotel days; there would have been a doorman dressed to the nines welcoming you inside with a big smile, and a concierge and bellhop stumbling over themselves that they couldn't shake your hand fast enough. Once upon a time, the lights in here were like a Hollywood marquee sign, and the red carpet rolled to every room.

Of course, that was an era ago. Les Deux Oies was like anything else in life; given enough time, it had faded to become a shadow of its original self, the days of newness and vitality long gone and nearly forgotten. The apartment building was no more than a piece of secondhand junk found inside someone's piece of lost baggage. Original gold leaf along the wall trim could still be seen, though now it cracked and peeled away like the hide of a dead animal. Light bulbs and bad wiring needed replacing, the wallpaper sagged, pipes leaked, and carpet stank.

Ah, who was I kidding? I condemned the building for being decrepit, when I was in the same condition. If ever a kettle called the pot black, it was me. Les Deux Oies was a good home, like an old used shoe that, once broken in, trades its shiny gloss for comfort and familiarity. I felt like I belonged here; it was something I'd grown with over the past decade. Together we'd weathered its ups and downs and begun the final descent into crumbling obscurity.

Yet I *wanted* more...I *wanted* to belong with Gail. It had been a long time since I hoped for something better for myself.

Going to New York could be for me what renovations were to Les Deux Oies: a new start. Deep down inside, though, I felt I didn't deserve it. The self-doubt gnawed at me...life was so fleeting, so *cold*. It was a mockery to imagine happiness. A voice whispered of meaning beyond what life offered...

I shuddered and got up and went outside to call Ray's shop again. I let the phone ring twenty times and was about to hang up, when someone finally answered.

"Yeah?" The voice made no effort to hide its aggravation.

"Hi, is this John?" I asked.

"What of it?"

"This is Charlie Stewart. We met at the auction."

"Oh, hey. Little late to need something, isn't it?"

"I'm looking for Ray. Is he over there?"

"Ain't seen him since yesterday. Want me to take a message?"

"Do you know where he could be? It's urgent I find him."

"Last I heard he went to your place. Didn't he show up?"

My heart sank. I had feared this. "Yeah, he was here, but he went back to the shop."

"Nobody's been here all night."

"You sure?"

"He hasn't been here. If you need something else, spit it out. I've got inventory to complete."

Vkhodite.

The word sounded so clear that I thought John spoke it through the phone. I slammed the handset against the cradle and returned inside.

If Ray never arrived at his shop, I knew where he wound up instead. Time was running out, and I prepared myself to return; I would have to end this horror alone.

This time going up the elevator, I heard the music begin to form earlier. Its amorphous essence hummed louder as I passed the third floor, filling in the silence between each click of the conveyor's ratcheting gears. The records' range was spreading. I dug into my pocket and pulled out the ear plugs Gail had given me. With them jammed into my ears, the world fell silent.

I reached the fourth floor and got out, immediately feeling the temperature drop in the hallway. A puff of wind blew along the corridor, and I thought of how many dozens of jackets I had in my room and that I should go up there and get one.

No, I thought. *If I left now, I might not have the strength to return.* I made my way to Joey's room.

His apartment was about ten rooms down from the elevator bank. I had walked the distance a thousand times before, but never before with this sense of dread. Every footfall moved in slow motion, and the distance seemed to triple. I passed two doors that were left wide open, Joey's neighbors who walked out and never returned. As I drew closer, the air grew colder still. I reached his home and didn't bother to knock. A scrim of snow and ice bordered the doorframe, and icicles hung off the knob.

I went inside.

After all I had seen over the past week, all I experienced—the craziness, the horror, the fear—I was still taken aback at the absurd changes before me.

There was no far wall to the apartment. Instead, the room acted as a clearing and, past it, were gnarled, intertwined limbs of giant pine trees that hinted at a great span of distance beyond. The living room and the stacks of baggage and collectibles were all still there but buried under a foot or more of white snow. The gramophone sat atop a stack of luggage, like an idol upon its alter, surrounded by a ring of fire. Bands of smoke circled upwards, and I saw that Joey's apartment no longer had a ceiling; it was roofed only by a shower of stars twinkling across the dead-black sky.

Ray was there, kneeling at the record player. I saw, too, Yefim and Horace Wetzel prostate before the machine. There were more—ten? fifteen?—new men, women, and children in the group, though I knew immediately Joey was not amongst them. If my heart were of glass, it would have shattered at the realization he was gone; there was no coming back from wherever he'd been taken. Joey Third had made his last gamble, and I knew it was a losing hand.

Even as I mourned Joey, I registered what other changes had recently occurred. Most of the people I saw earlier in the day were also gone, or replaced, including the Scandinavian, Martin, and his wife. The woman with blue hair was still there, but she was as I saw Joey last: a fleeting shadow glimpsed within Rasputin, like the image of a movie projector upon the screen. There were more records stacked by the gramophone, too, more than originally came in the suitcase.

*The second voice is different on each album...*I remembered Joey telling me in the lobby. Were there more records because more souls had been *recorded* on each? As Vic explained, their voices were unlocking the realms of immortality through the chants. I shuddered, wondering where that immortality would be spent.

A teenage boy with unruly hair and zits on his chin stood from the group and walked into the forest, singing like he was performing an encore at the *Grand Ole Opry*. The tree limbs parted as he passed and then snapped back into place as if he'd never been there.

Rasputin opened his arms to me, expecting my surrender. I stood my ground, frozen by fear as much as by the cold. The door opened from behind, and an Oriental woman wearing a housedress lurched inside.

She passed me, walking through the snow to the fire, and I read the single word she mouthed on her lips. *Vkhodite.*

Rasputin smiled and said something in return. I could only guess as to his reply: *Ne zaderzhivat'sya v kholodnyy i temnyy...*

People were passing through this room as if it were a way station. He was calling them, through the music, attracting more followers that he…what? Consumed? Assimilated? What happened to Joey and the others, where did they go?

Another gust of wind blew across the room, and the trees rustled. In that movement, their branches parted, and I saw another clearing, another campfire, far off in the distance. People were there, and I saw the singing teenage boy sit down. Behind that were the fairy-tale castles of my dreams. It was a world *within* a world, much as I saw Joey and the blue-haired woman as people *within* people, perhaps a mirror image of the reality I used to believe or, perhaps, the echoes of another time. Rasputin was calling his followers, the Misbegottens, to action.

What had happened to the real Rasputin? What had he attempted before his death? The book about him was back up in my room, and I thought of the answers it might hold.

Rasputin still looked at me, speaking, from behind the record player and campfire. How long would it take until he comprehended I couldn't hear him, that his words held no effect while I wore the ear plugs?

I rushed forward, each footfall sinking deeper into the drifts of snow. I grabbed Ray from behind and wrestled him up, trying to haul his limp weight backwards and out the room. The Oriental woman had sat behind Ray, and she blocked the return path. The campfire sparked upwards, and the woman reached over and tore at my face with her nails. Her eyes were blank, and her movement was as if a reflex, such as stepping on a dead cat's paw will cause its claws to extend out.

I recoiled away from the scratching woman, and Ray slipped from my hold. I tried to lift him again but he was bigger than me, and it was difficult to navigate in the snow. He began to struggle, batting away my arms, then turned and struck me with his fist. I fell to my knees in the snow though, with its depth, it was almost like falling to my waist. I struggled to stand, and the others around the campfire rose and moved toward me. The Oriental woman lunged again, but this time I was ready. She was skinnier than a thermometer, so I just shoved her, and she fell backwards on her keister.

The others came at me but, they too, had difficulty advancing through the snowdrift. Also they moved slow and stiff, as if they had boards tied to their limbs and tried to walk across a tightrope. I could evade them one-by-one, but I didn't want to find out what would happen if they got hold of me as a group.

I scrambled out through the snowdrift, which became shallower as it sloped down to the door, until I found the icy footing of the apartment floor. I ran out the doorway into the hall, and a swirl of flakes billowed after me. A tenant I recognized—Mr. Landis, a widower from the fifth floor— walked toward me from the elevators, head rocking side-to- side. He was the oldest person in the building, with a face like a piece of dried fruit: wrinkled and weathered and colored like something you would find on a moldy plate. He limped by with a cane, and I prepared to bowl him over if he reached for me. But Landis just passed and shuffled into Joey's room.

I saw his lips move: *vkhodite*.

I ran to the elevators. Again. I had run more in the past week than I had all the rest of the year added up. Leave it to a life-threatening horror to give you a real workout. I waited for the doors to open and felt that music tugging at me. Even with the ear plugs, it was still working itself into my brain. I didn't know how much longer I could fight it. Rasputin's effect was truly spreading; if sound traveled outwards in equal radiance, the tenants on the third floor would be just as brainwashed as those on the fifth. After that it would move to the second and sixth…There were over a hundred people living in the building and all could soon become the Mad Monk's sacrifices.

Once the elevator arrived, I punched in "six" and rode it to my floor. I bounded out and dashed to my room. I shouldn't have expected differently, but was relieved to find everything as I left it earlier in the day, when accompanied by Yefim and Ray.

The night fell late, and starlight filtered into the room. The summer temperature sank lower than it had any right to. It tolled midnight, and I knew not if that had any bearing on Rasputin's power, but considered it another poor omen, stacking in his favor like the fact of the moon being full.

Time, time, time—it was always against me. Following Murphy's law of nature: apparently when circumstances are dire, the clock will move twice as fast. As it was, the limitations of time already seemed to crop up at the worst of circumstances to interfere with my intentions. I knew I was running even more on its bad side now and aware that Rasputin grew stronger, while I deteriorated like decaying leaves.

I had to act fast. I picked up the book of Rasputin, ready to read like my life depended on it...which it did. At this point, I didn't know how much of what had been written was fact or assumption or bald-faced lie, but I didn't have the luxury of being finicky. I had to trust every word and pray the answers popped their heads up to say *howdy*. There was nothing else to go on.

I opened to the dog-eared page where I had earlier left off...

Dark whispers circulated amongst Rasputin's chief followers of which I was privy. He was said to have gained access to another realm in which to escape and grow strong, one which he froze in time, mirroring the Black Forest outside Saint Petersburg where his rituals were practiced. The Misbegottens gathered every full moon at midnight to recite Rasputin's incantations.

His followers sought life beyond death, a continuation of existence in which they believed. Otherwise, preached Rasputin, the soul simply winked out like a failed bulb once the body died. His words were persuasive, nay, magical, and those who listened were easily converted. I found myself in that belief, though a part of me—a fragment of mind still filled with the holy spirit—knew that the immortality Rasputin spoke of was not for all. Rasputin took the souls of his followers for his own use, so their bodies were nothing but shambling husks submissive to his whim. I know not how many souls Rasputin required to achieve the perpetuity he sought, if the number was predetermined or required a steady flow, such as the need for sustenance once hunger strikes.

If I hadn't experienced what I did over the past week, I would've thought this book garbage, filled with the gleeful rantings of a nutcase. Again I was struck by how the perceptions of man can change so rapidly, so *dramatically*, within such a short period of time. What else that I believed so fervently was untrue? What else was possible that I considered absurd? I was prepared to nod my head if someone came up to me and said they were the demon, Zolga, teleported from a Mars brothel. I skipped ahead in the book, and what I read next, I almost wished I hadn't.

In 1915, Rasputin acquired a gramophone, a model with no identification or manufacturer's markings. Though he had written certain words in ink to be repeated by his followers, the chants were not enough. He said that his abilities ebbed and flowed like the tides of the Baltic Sea, as those who sang his name paused during song. The human condition requires respite, which Rasputin abhorred. The gramophone, however, could play his chants forever.

Somehow, through magic or trickery, he found a new manner in which to ingurgitate the life flow of his converts. On special discs that were crafted by a shadow, Rasputin recorded the voices of his Misbegottens one-by-one. I was present at such a recording session, and at what horror I witnessed was enough to break the spell over which Rasputin had chained me. Music played in the air, but as to its source I saw none. I watched a woman sit upon her knees and chant to him perhaps a hundred times:

Vkhodite. Vkhodite. Vkhodite.

Ne zaderzhivat'sya v kholodnyy i temnyy, ho prisoyedinit'sya ko mne v svet navsegda.

Vkhodite. Vkhodite. Vkhodite.

At each recital of those words, her body paled and faded, ever-so-slightly. But it was a compound effort, so that over time she literally faded away until there existed nothing but her voice, playing continually on the gramophone. She had been 'recorded' for all eternity. At that, Rasputin glowed a ruddy hue, such as one who has imbibed a great deal of red wine on a cold night.

I felt nauseated. A heavy sickness filled my belly and spread so that every nerve cried out until I thought I would faint again. I fought to remain conscious. It was the nightmare I had lived, watching the records take Joey and the others away. Had I known earlier what I knew now, what could I have done differently? Take the record player from Joey by force? I thought, somehow, that wouldn't have changed a thing. Once Rasputin's gramophone had been turned on, there was no shutting it off.

But Rasputin was dead...he hadn't succeeded in his quest for immortality before. How had he been defeated?

During the last eighteen months of Rasputin's life, several assassination attempts were made on him, including stabbings, explosives, and gassings. He survived them all. Finally, on December 29, 1916, a group of nobles conspired together that Rasputin must be destroyed, lest all their own lives and families fall victim to his corrupted persuasions. Led by Prince Felix Yusupov and Grand Duke Dmitri Pavlovich, Rasputin was invited to a ceremony and served cakes and red wine laced with "enough cyanide to kill ten men." Reportedly, he was not affected. Prince Yusupov drew a revolver and shot Rasputin in the back. Bolstered by Yusupov's act, other conspirators also drew and shot Rasputin until "no less than eight

*bullets were fired into his torso." Reportedly, he still was not affected
and strangled Yusupov to death.*

I thought sarcastically, *isn't that keen*. Of course the Mad
Monk was invulnerable to most methods normally used to
overcome a man. I continued:

*Fortunately, Pavlovich had apparently studied Rasputin and
previously unearthed a weakness. He drew a club carved from
limestone and beat Rasputin to the ground, until the others could
subdue and bind his limbs. He was gagged and wrapped in a carpet
and then thrown off a bridge into the icy Neva River. Rasputin was
conscious and struggling to the end. His body was recovered three
days later, and the official autopsy declared the sole cause of death as
drowning.*

    *I approached Pavlovich some years later and inquired discreetly
as to the club. 'Calcium carbonate,' he replied. It is the most abundant
mineral found in water. Calcium, in composite, forms limestone.
Though not lethal, it was an infirmity to Rasputin, an indicator of his
true vulnerability:*

    Drowning.

I remembered reading earlier: *Rasputin's siblings died by
drowning-effects, and he nearly drowned himself. After his rescue is
when he began to portray indications of supernatural powers.*

Water, somehow, intertwined with his life, and drowning
was apparently the one weakness of the Mad Monk since his
childhood. But how could I drown him on the fourth floor of
an apartment building?

Or, perhaps, the key wasn't in Rasputin himself...

I needed tools and weapons, and I looked around my
apartment. I'd never felt more vindicated of my baggage
winnings than at that very moment. Anything I needed to
defeat Rasputin, I knew was at hand, as if I'd been
subconsciously stockpiling all these years in an effort to protect

Les Deux Oies. There simply wasn't anything I *didn't* have. The challenge, of course, would be in actually locating such items stored amidst the towers of castoffs.

I began searching. I was shivering cold and getting colder still, so the first item of business was to change out of my dinner suit and into warmer clothes: two layers of pants, several wool flannels, a sailor's peacoat, and boots. I thought of the locker I had, filled with equipment that once belonged to an Everest mountaineer.

Snowshoes. I rummaged through the piles and came out with a used pair made from wood and bound in rawhide. If Joey's brainwashed neighbors still sat around the fire in drifts of snow, I could at least now easily outmaneuver them. I slung the shoes over my shoulder. The locker was also crammed with pick axes, compasses, goggles, stakes, and other unfamiliar gear that smelled of mildew and old age. A leather bag of powdered chalk hung jammed into a corner; I hesitated, then tied it to my belt by its drawstring.

I saw my prized conquistador's sword and pistol hanging on hooks above a pile of bags filled with cushions and linen. The pistol wouldn't be of any use, but whoever owned the sword before me had kept it oiled and sharp and in otherwise exquisite condition. I lifted it, and the sword felt good in my hand. It looked to be as lethal as anything else in the room, so I hooked the scabbard to my belt opposite the chalk bag, hoping I wouldn't need to use it.

*What else...*I wished the original plan had gone through, and I headed to the room alongside Ray, armed with guns. Not that I was a sharpshooter, but I'd hunted a bit as a kid in Kentucky and would have preferred going into any conflict holding a Colt .45 or Browning. As to what else I could use for a weapon, my eyes scanned the room and landed on a Louisville slugger baseball bat. As good as the sword had felt in my hand, the bat felt *natural*. I'd swung a bat a thousand times for every instance I'd touched a sword.

I realized how ridiculous I must have looked: a baseball-playing conquistador dressed to hike in the snow. But everything had a purpose. I thought of also bringing the book with me but realized there would be no time to read as I ventured downstairs. I was already heavily burdened, and anything else would be detrimental, adding to my load. I was never a quick student but hoped I remembered, and *understood*, everything I'd read in its pages.

I felt as prepared as I could be given the circumstances. I considered that, should the first part of my plan inexplicably succeed, I'd need an escape from Les Deux Oies as quick as possible. Of course I remembered the Crestline was out of commission, and escaping quick wouldn't happen without the participation of someone else. It was late in the night...who could I beseech to act as a getaway driver? Who, *besides* Gail, as I didn't want to involve her further? Could I call John at Ray's shop again? He was supposed to be there all night, but could I convince him of what had occurred? He'd think I was in my room gettin' plastered.

I pulled out the ear plugs and tried John. After thirty rings, I hung up. I called Vic, though I knew he went to bed at dusk. No answer. I even rang up my bookie. No dice. I considered just calling a cabbie, but decided how ridiculously unreliable they were; even more so than me.

There really wasn't much of another option available. Either I tried to hotfoot it out of here for ten miles on my tired dogs, or I got a car ride from Gail.

I reluctantly called her, and Gail answered on the first ring.

"Hello?" she said.

"It's me."

"Is it over? Are you all right?"

"No, dear, not quite." I wanted to say, *it's worse*. Instead I kept my tone even without letting the fears slip through. "It'll be over soon. I do need a favor, though."

"Anything."

"I need you to drive me away from the apartments."

"You just need a ride? That's all?"

Oh, but what a ride it will be, I thought. I asked, "How long until you could get here?"

"I'm ready to leave now, so give me twenty minutes' drive time."

"Pull up to the curb outside the front entrance and keep the engine running."

She paused. "Is there anything else I should know, Charlie?"

I evaded the question. "I'm counting on you being here in twenty minutes. I'll be waiting. If I'm not outside already, wait five minutes for me and then leave. Just get far away, all the way to New York, and don't look back."

"You're scaring me. Why don't I wait as long as it takes for you to get ready?"

"If I'm not out there in time, something will have happened. Something, that if you came looking for me, would affect you, too...the ghost of Rasputin..."

"When have you ever been on time for anything? I'm not leaving you up there."

"Please, Gail. Just do as I ask. I've got enough to worry about without fretting over your safety."

She sighed, a long and deep sound as if a wind blew through the receiver. "Okay, Charlie. I'll be there in twenty minutes and I won't wait around."

"Thank you. And, Gail...bring ear plugs for yourself."

"I will."

On impulse, I added, "And New York sounds like a wonderful idea."

"Are you saying you'll go with me?"

"I'm just saying what I'm saying. It's a wonderful idea. If circumstances were different I'd be there in a flash. As it is...I don't know what's going to happen tonight."

"You'll pull through. You always land on your feet. Think positive, of a new life for us."

I didn't want to think of anything but surviving the next hour. "I gotta go. If all goes to plan, I'll meet you downstairs."

"I'll see you, Charlie. I know I will. I love you."

"Love you too, Gail."

I hung up, questioning if I did the right thing. My life—my soul—were already at stake…even if she was my only hope, should I have asked her for assistance and put her at risk as well? I pushed it out of my mind. *Stay positive*, I thought, just like Gail told me. Unfortunately, I wasn't very adept at positivity.

I looked around the room one last time, hoping to draw on an inner strength found through happy memories of days lounging on the phone with collectors and nights opening baggage with Joey. Regardless of what was to happen, I knew that part of my life was closed; nothing would ever return to the way it was.

I left my apartment and walked slowly down the hall to the elevator bank. Each step felt planned by someone other than me, like a force pulling my legs closer to it, one-at-a-time. I entered the conveyor, and that same force brought my arm up to punch the fourth floor button. I still wore the ear plugs Gail gave me, but I imagined the music playing anyway in my mind. Already my thoughts began to jumble…was it truly my imagination or did I actually hear it? Rasputin must have realized I was less susceptible to his chants when I went in after Ray. Would he double his efforts to convert me, or did he possess other facilities with which to subdue me?

I read in Rasputin's biography that he could foretell the future…I trembled, wondering if that were true and if he waited down there prepared, knowing exactly what I intended to do. I thought that, at least, he couldn't be at the height of his power, as he was still collecting souls, still passing through the transition process.

The elevator reached the fourth floor, and I exited, pausing outside its door. The hallway before me seemed to stretch away like a narrow cobblestone lane. Snowflakes and dead leaves swirled alongside the molding, and the apartment doors appeared as hollows cut into dense groves of trees. But it appeared, too, as a simple beige hallway, covered in cheap carpet that led to Joey's room. Again I felt that sense of two worlds overlapping each other, as if one existed within the other and bulged out, overflowing its confines.

A chrome ashtray stand squatted in the corner of the hall. I took it and placed it in the elevator entrance, so that the door could not close and the conveyor descend. I walked. The same force that seemed to pull me along since I left my room now felt more urgent, more *in control*. As I approached Joey's room, the force warmed me, and I felt a flush of confidence. I realized what propelled me forward was nothing nefarious, but instead a certain stimulus. It inspired me that what I was to attempt was for "good," if good and bad could be so easily delineated. When I heard reports of heroics performed by everyday people they often remarked that whatever occurred had gone against their normal nature; they acted on impulse. I could only hope such a noble consciousness was leading me at this time.

In moments I was there, standing outside Joey's door. I grasped the knob and my skin stuck to the frozen metal. I turned it, and tiny icicles shattered within the tumbler. The door was difficult to open as the hinges were likewise frozen, and as I pushed against it with all my might, I saw that I pushed the door into an ever-deepening drift of snow.

Vkhodite.

The bad voice came back, and my sense of noble consciousness went the way of the dinosaurs. I made enough space between the door and the snow that I could slip through.

What had once been Joey's apartment could no longer be called as such. Whereas the last time I entered, the far wall had given way to dense forests, now, too, did all the other confines of the room. I shivered in a clearing carved from woods, and in all directions the trees pressed together like interlocking fingers. The doorway I passed from stood as a singular object unattached to anything but the ground, the way a gravestone thrusts from the earth.

Rasputin and the converts were gone.

I knew I entered the realm the book spoke of: the land of Black Forest, frozen in time outside Saint Petersburg. Though I felt relief at his absence, part of me panicked. I had to find the record player fast. The fire still burned in the ground ahead, though the flames were low, its strength waning from the falling snow and lack of fuel. The suitcases that had served as altar for the record player were toppled over, and a group of footprints led away through the trees. He'd led them to the original clearing, where the Misbegottens once gathered for his worship.

Though all the walls and ceiling were gone, Joey's belongings remained, half-buried under snow. To my left his dining table tilted up as if an ice wave pushed from beneath. Greasy plates had slid off and piled in a heap to one side, and I saw the remains of breakfast I had brought him earlier that morning. A full day hadn't passed since our last conversation, though it seemed a lifetime ago. Rasputin's transformation was accelerating.

To my right were heaps of Joey's baggage, tumbled in disarray, but I quickly located the leather suitcase under a scrim of pale snow. Apparently nobody thought twice of it; the case numbered just one of hundreds of luggage items stored throughout the apartment. Perhaps I was wrong and it held no significance, but I wagered my life that the suitcase was the only way to contain the record player. I made my way to it and immediately began to sink to my knees in the deepening snow.

I sat down to put on the snowshoes. Never having worn them before, I lashed the shoes to my feet as best I could and was amazed that they worked better than hoped. Though my steps were awkward, I no longer sank when I walked. I made my way to the leather suitcase and broke it free from the others. With the knowledge of what I now looked for, I reexamined the handle and strange stones lining the seams of the case. I rubbed my fingers over the texture, and they felt hard and rough, not smooth like ivory which I first assumed it to be. The slight greenish hue veining the stones confirmed my belief: *limestone*. As the book described, it was antithetical to Rasputin.

Still holding the baseball bat in one hand, I took the case in the other, and walked across the clearing, following the footprints. They entered the forest, and I pursued, pushing with effort through snarling limbs. The trees were high altitude perennials, Siberian pines and junipers, and they grew close together like clumps of grass. I thought that those who walked before me must have broken through the branches already so that I would follow a cleared path, but the limbs seemed flexible, rubbery, and they snapped back into place rather than cracking off.

After a dozen yards I looked back and could no longer see the clearing I had entered from. The forest was a world of itself, a trap where one might wander lost for eternity; there were no identifying features, and even the night sky overhead didn't make sense. Where I knew the Big Dipper and Orion constellations should be present, instead shone distant pulsating orbs, smaller than the moon but expanding and contracting like the beating of a heart. Had I not the footprints to follow, I would have no hope of finding my way through. As it was, snow still fell from the sky, and the prints were gradually fading as I watched.

I hurried onward. I wanted to run, but the snowshoes made that impossible. Instead, I made long, wide steps and trusted that I moved faster than those I pursued. I was proved correct as the footprints became deeper, fresher. Soon, I saw the first figure ahead, his back to me as he stumbled and labored to march through the snow, following at a far distance from someone else.

I still wore the ear plugs, but could imagine the converts' voices, chanting in mantra as they walked. I pushed through the tree limbs with urgency and, as I grew closer to the figure, saw he leaned precariously on a cane, struggling to keep up with the others.

Mr. Landis, the oldest tenant in Les Deux Oies.

I silently asked for forgiveness and hoped that I caused him no other harm, if there was anything left of his original self which *could* be harmed. I set the suitcase down and swung the Louisville Slugger into the back of his head. I only used half my strength, but Landis crumpled like a wet bag.

I picked up the suitcase and hurried past him. Fifty yards further, I came upon the next person, the Oriental woman wearing a housedress who had blocked me from dragging Ray out of the room. Like Landis, she had her back to me and paid no notice as I crept from behind. My first thought was to wonder how she walked through the snow in just a dress without turning into a Popsicle. I supposed that in whatever state their mind existed was part of Rasputin's spiritual transcendence, and the effects of the physical world didn't affect them. I swung the baseball bat into her skull and she fell. Whatever transcendence they experienced, they were still affected by blunt-force trauma.

In front of her was another man, blindly following in the footprints of those in front of him, like a dumb trail of ants. I felled him with the bat. The orbs in the sky pulsed brighter, and the trees thinned slightly, and the land sloped downward, so that all combined allowed me a faraway glimpse of the *other* campfire. I knew this was the axis of Rasputin's realm, that which I had glimpsed from Joey's room. The fire there roared in a geyser of flame, surrounded by scores of shadowy figures kneeling in rows. Rasputin was bringing the record player home, leading the newest converts from Les Deux Oies.

I had no other plan but to move forward, approaching sleepwalking people from behind and braining them as if I were a back-alley hood. They were so single-minded in their trek not one noticed my approach. I wasn't normally much of a slugger, but in these circumstances, I was doing all right. I probably could have stood face-to-face and, unless Rasputin commanded otherwise, they still wouldn't have lifted a finger to protect themselves. As it was, I preferred clonking them from behind...I didn't want to see the walking-coma faces of people I once chatted with.

I came upon two women struggling through the snow, each step sinking them to their knees, and I felled them. Rasputin either didn't know, or care, that I was toppling his victims. As long as the music played, they moved forward. Perhaps I headed into a trap and Rasputin knew I would be one of his soon enough...or, perhaps, he simply didn't expect anyone to follow him into his own world.

Ahead, I saw the record player, and my heart skipped more than a beat. Two men carried it reverently between them, stepping in tandem. Even from a distance, I saw the black disc spinning beneath the needle and could imagine its music, that horrible cacophony of instruments screeching together.

I raced as quickly to them as the snowshoes would allow. I imagined chopping down a tree, and I hit each man in the back of the head with consecutive swings. *Thwack. Thwack.* The gramophone fell into the snow, still playing.

A knife of words slashed across my thoughts. *Stoy! Predatel!*

The alarm had sounded. I saw the figures farther up the trail turn and scuttle toward me. The ant line was broken. They were coming for me any way they could, and I knew that included the Misbegottens from the distant campfire. They moved through the drifts as if in slow motion, lifting legs comically high while trying to traverse the snow. Rasputin would be among them, and I had only fleeting moments before they arrived.

I set the suitcase next to the gramophone and opened it wide. The record seemed to spin faster on the turntable as if frantically trying to hypnotize me before I confined it. If the gramophone had legs, it would have scrambled away like a spider about to get squashed. I picked it up, and the sides of the wooden base scalded my hands. I cried out and heaved it into the empty suitcase. Normally, when a record player is jostled, the arm slides and scratches the record all to hell. Not this one. It still played fine as a dancehall juke. Steam sizzled from my burned flesh, but I ignored the pain and slammed the suitcase closed. The limestone edges lined up at the seams, and for the first time I noticed that they formed a pattern leading away from each side of the handle in a series of abstract crosses. I didn't have time to examine it.

I ran.

I ran, the way a man might run who wore clown shoes, twenty sizes too large. Retreating through the woods was no easier than advancing forward only minutes earlier. One might think the way back would be less arduous, the path having been broken in. But, instead, the tree branches now seemed sturdier, less pliable to bend out of the way, yet too tough to be broken. Indeed, they seemed almost as living creatures reaching to ensnare me with contorted fingers. I dropped the baseball bat and held the suitcase with both hands, using it as a shield in front of me to push through the forest.

Stoy! Stoy!

The voice screamed in my mind, ordering me to stop, and I slowed, feeling compelled to obey. Fortunately another part of me took over. It was a part that I—like most rational people—normally kept shackled deep down in the recesses of my persona. The part that, when you're at a bar and someone spills their drink on you, wants to leap out and throttle the drunken slob. The part that, when you're handed the bill from an auto mechanic and see you're grossly overcharged, wants to slap the deceitful swindler and stuff the bill down his throat. It was the part of me that was wild with inconsequence and once outraced a cop car and another time taunted a rabid dog.

That part of me told Rasputin to kick a turd. That part of me said to keep running.

I then felt that nothing would stop me. Rasputin's voice in my brain grew louder, but I ignored it. It repeated in severity, but I knew not to stop. It got closer, so that I felt a tingle creeping up the back of my neck, like the breath of his words tickling my skin. I knew it was only in my head, but I still turned expecting the Mad Monk to be alongside, shouting right into my ears. Though I saw pursuing figures, there was nobody immediately near. I turned back, and a branch cracked into my forehead...It wasn't me *running into* a branch; the tree limb swung across the path like pulling a car antenna sideways all the way and letting go. I clunked backwards, and my feet went over my head. Flashing stars exploded, brighter than the lights twinkling in the night.

Shouts and curses and strange squeals sounded through the air. I realized I could hear again, and the ear plugs were knocked loose. But the music wasn't playing; being locked up in the suitcase was apparently enough to keep it turned off. I was comforted it wouldn't brainwash me, but maybe it didn't matter...Rasputin's voice was still in my head.

Stoy! Predatel!

I staggered back to my feet and knew Rasputin and his followers were closing in. How much further had I to go? I lifted the suitcase back up and pushed on through the trees, wary of their limbs swaying back-and-forth the way a cobra warns before it strikes. A couple more times they took a swing, but I dodged away. My legs were heavy, and my breath erupted in irregular gasps. The pulsating orbs in the sky grew larger like frightened eyes, and the snow fell harder. It became difficult to see more than five feet in front of me, but I pushed forward, head down, concentrating on following my tracks back to the door.

I strained and labored and fought my way back up the path and through the trees until, with an exhausted roar, I broke through, falling into the clearing. The campfire was nothing but smoldering gray ash, and most of the suitcases looked like ice sculptures. The door was still cracked open as I left it, though slowly vanishing under the snow flurries.

To my right, the trees parted easily as fluttering curtains, almost as if they bowed to passing royalty. Rasputin emerged, calmly striding with long steps to come between me and the apartment door.

But it wasn't just Rasputin. It was Ray, *within* Rasputin, looking at me through Ray's eyes that looked at me through Rasputin's eyes.

I was a goddamned war hero, those eyes seemed to say. *Look at me now.*

Then he spoke, and the voice was unmistakably that from the records.

"Vkhodite."

Rasputin snapped his fingers. I shuddered. A beat passed, and he snapped again. The corners of his lips pulled tight and the tips of his white teeth showed through. He snapped his fingers again in rhythm, as if there were a secret beat only he could hear.

"Yapobedit," he said. He snapped his fingers as Ray snapped his fingers, and I figured that Rasputin took on more than just the physical characteristics of those he absorbed.

I held the suitcase up, so its handle and limestone crosses pointed at him, like a talisman. Rasputin wavered, and he screwed up his face like something stunk real bad. The limestone was said to be antithetical to him, but I didn't know to what extent that meant. Did he simply dislike it, the way I detested cauliflower, or did limestone actually injure him? Rasputin grimaced and more of his teeth showed, then he closed his eyes and, with a shout, brought both hands down on the suitcase, knocking it from my hands. A bit of steam floated from his skin where it touched the case, but it was no more than how the record player had burned me. *Touché.*

Of course the suitcase fell closer to him than to me, and when Rasputin opened his eyes, I saw how much that pleased him. I wouldn't be able to grab it before he took hold of me. I wanted to slice off the smile that grew on his face, so I drew the conquistador's sword from my belt.

I swung at him the way Errol Flynn might have done, in a wide, swashbuckling arc. Being as I've never struck a sword at someone before, it shouldn't have surprised me that I missed completely. Instead of advancing, my confidence waned, and I stepped back to reappraise the situation.

Rasputin's features melted, swirling, like colors of different wax running upon each other. The mask of Ray's face was gone, and Rasputin's own showed clearly, solidly, before that too melted and then reappeared as before, a face within a face. The new face was of a woman, and I recognized her as the gorgeous wife of the Scandinavian, Martin. She wasn't so gorgeous now, but it was her, a photograph of life existing in a false vessel.

I didn't know if he was showing off or trying to intimidate me, or some law in his world required he change form every so often. Maybe he thought I wouldn't strike a woman. I wouldn't let niceties stop me now.

I pointed the sword at him, ready to charge again. "This is for Joey."

I expected him to reply with his usual '*Vkhodite,*' but he only glared at me. What he did next tormented me more than anything else he might have said, anyway. Rasputin's face melted again, and Joey's appeared. His lips pursed together and his cheeks rose, the way they would when Joey acted mischievous. I shouldn't have voiced Joey's name; all that did was give Rasputin new ideas of what to use against me.

"*Vkhodite*," he said. There it was, the word I expected, only this time it was Joey speaking to me, and I imagined: *Come in, Charlie. It's time to come in.*

"You're nothin' but a broken record," I said. I thrust the sword forward in a straight line—no fancy arc—and it sunk dead-center into Rasputin's chest.

After all that, the sword ended up not doing a thing to help, and I got the sense Rasputin was toying with me. He shrugged the attack off and stood there with it sticking out of him like a third arm. I thought back to the stories I'd read of him: Rasputin had been stabbed, shot, poisoned, and none of that affected him. Why would it be any different now? Joey's face looked down at me and his head shook, like I was the one to be pitied and not him.

The trees began to open up, and I saw glimpses of people about to pass through into the clearing. I had to act now. Rasputin reached his right hand across the hilt of the sword and began to pull it out of his chest. I leapt forward and grabbed at the suitcase near his feet. Rasputin reached for me with his other hand, as I thought he would.

He couldn't grab me. Rasputin fumbled and looked at his hand as if it betrayed him, but I knew otherwise. He wore people like a layer of clothes, and part of him took on their physical characteristics. While he maintained Joey's form, his left hand was useless as a shoe full of mud. Those broken fingers couldn't do a thing but poke at me. It was a good thing, too, because when they brushed against my neck, his fingers were colder than anything I could have imagined, as if the deepest reaches of the Arctic Ocean drained into that hand. I shudder to imagine what would have happened if it could have wrapped around my throat.

I stepped away from him, triumphant, holding the suitcase once again, though Rasputin still stood before the door, and now he brandished the sword against me. On the flipside of our circumstances, I knew a sword strike would harm me plenty. I still felt the icy touch of Rasputin's hand on my neck, and it seemed the skin where he touched turned dead from frostbite. The first of the Misbegottens pushed through the trees at the clearing, tromping high through the deep snow.

I dug my hand into the mountaineer's bag of powdered chalk I carried on my belt and came out with a handful. I didn't have any wisecracking final words to add, so I just flung the dust into Rasputin's face, aiming for his eyes.

He shook his head once, about annoyed as if a horsefly meandered past. Then something changed. His mouth unhinged, and his eyes turned even bigger than they usually appeared. Rasputin screwed up his face and shrieked like a nest of hornets had been let loose in his pants. His eyes closed tight and little wisps of smoke plumed up. He whipped the sword at me quick but, blinded, his aim was even more lopsided than my Errol Flynn swing.

Limestone *did* hurt Rasputin. Maybe not permanently, but enough to slow him down. I don't know how I remembered such a thing but chalk, after all, is simply ground-up calcium carbonate. *Powdered limestone.*

I dodged to one side and ran around him and squeezed through the apartment door. I hit that hallway running, but after two steps tripped over the snowshoes and went sprawling. The carpet burn was almost as bad as the shame. I heard crashing and shouts coming from the other side of Joey's room. I frantically worked at the straps holding the snowshoes onto my feet, but my fingers were numb from the cold and everything I tried took twice as long as it should with half the result.

"Stoy! Predatel!"

The voices were muffled, but they were close. Worse, I couldn't tell if they were from Joey's room or in my head or a little of both. My sight was fading from my peripheral vision, and something felt to be pushing against my guts, and I imagined Rasputin trying to force his way inside my body.

Finally the snowshoes fell off, and I ran in a staggering bounce-off-the-wall pace until I got in the elevator. I kicked the chrome ashtray aside and, as the doors closed, I saw figures stumbling out of Joey's apartment.

That elevator ride down four floors was the longest of my life. I considered how vulnerable I'd be if caught in that narrow metal box. Already the walls seemed to close in, and snow somehow followed me inside.

Stoy! Stoy!

That was definitely in my head. I cried out for the inner strength that had rescued me before to come back, but it must have been on coffee break.

Ne zaderzhivat'sya v kholodnyy i temnyy...

I shook my head back-and-forth like a lunatic, talking to myself. "No, no, go away, you're not real."

Finally the elevator reached bottom, and I tottered out into the lobby. It appeared as an ice castle, the floor shimmering blue-and-white and the broken couches arranged as a series of thrones. I heard echoes of voices chasing me from all directions. Shadows watched and grew from the corners like a pack of uneasy dogs, gathering courage to attack in number. I walked through it all, letting memory guide me along; I'd strolled through the lobby of Les Deux Oies every day for over a decade. My vision was filled with falling snow, and I felt something crackling in my brain, something else strangling my throat. I gasped and staggered and forced each leg to take a step forward. I don't know how I made it out the front entrance, but soon enough I pushed through the lobby doors into Detroit's early dawning sky.

Gail was there, waiting. A tiny part of my mind—that clock-watching sense of guilt—screamed at how late I was. Hadn't I told her twenty minutes, give or take? How had I been in Rasputin's world for so long? The sun was beginning to rise, and I knew I was hours behind what I said, but she had stayed. I could only imagine the worry and indecision gnawing away as she sat parked by the curb, watching the front door as each second ticked away. I knew, too, that if she hadn't waited—if she wasn't there that exact moment—I would have surrendered. I would have cried out in defeat and collapsed on the sidewalk that appeared so pale and empty like a sheet of ice.

As it was, I nearly collapsed anyway. But Gail came to me straight away, wrapping an arm around my shoulder, bearing my sagging weight, and guiding me to her car.

"Is that it? The record player?" she asked.

I had to look around for a moment before I realized I held what she was referring to.

My breaths were shallow, and I startled to hear how hoarse and slow my voice sounded. "Yes..."

"So what now?"

"The river," I said. "Detroit River. Take us over Ambassador Bridge."

My hands convulsed and fingers spasmed so that they turned into claws, but I would not let go of the suitcase. I sat down in the car seat, and my entire being screamed in relief. I wanted to close my eyes and let go, but I had to wait; this wasn't over yet. Gail drove us away.

It was about a ten-minute drive to Ambassador Bridge but, like everything, time seemed to skew, shrugging off the normal laws it should have abided by. Of all the moments it had sped past while I wasn't paying attention, this instance was the opposite; time threw me for a loop and slowed to a crawling second-by-second pace in which we drove as if the brakes were on. I could have relived my life twice over by the time we were a block down Sanford Street.

Come in, come in, the voice still whispered in my thoughts. Then: *Let me in, let me in...*

It took me a moment to realize that the voice was still speaking in Russian, yet I understood the words as if they were my native tongue.

"*Vkhodite,*" I said.

And I don't remember anything else about that drive or what happened afterwards on the bridge.

Chapter 8

Almost half a century has passed since that night, and time and I never really reconciled. In the same way that it's betrayed me so often by skipping ahead at the most inopportune moments, time has somehow now perpetrated the most reprehensible disservice of all. I find myself old and nostalgic, wondering at its tricks, and how so many years could have slipped by so quickly.

I'm told that time is a relative concept and everyone interprets it differently. I suppose that holds true because my interpretation of time on that drive to Ambassador Bridge really *was* skewed. Gail said I didn't start speaking Russian until we were already pulling onto the Bridge. The last thing I remember was that I had spoken Russian all my life.

Gail ended up being the real hero of this account. I may have found that proverbial cork to stick back into the genie's bottle, but she was the one who actually popped it in. Without Gail, I'd be nothing but a specter in Rasputin's forest, chanting for eternity alongside Joey and Ray and the others.

She said I frightened her like nobody's business once I started chanting. She drove for about a quarter mile across the river while I looked right at her and spoke a steady stream of Russian, as if I were trying to convince her of something. I popped the latches of the suitcase open, and she saw the gramophone moving inside, struggling like a dog locked in a cage that's too small.

That's when she pulled over.

The way Gail tells it, I put up a good fight. But like I said before, I hit like a pansy, and she beat the stuffing out of me, tearing that suitcase from my cold, curled fingers. I've even got a thin scar on my lip where she punched me with the small diamond ring I'd given her. To this day, I don't know how she knew to throw it in the river, and Gail still doesn't know either. Plain ol' woman's intuition, I guess. She closed the suitcase's latches again, just as the needle fell against a record and began to play. She took that case and heaved it with the strength of a dozen lumberjacks far over the railing and into the dark water below. It sank like an anchor and a puff of steam billowed up.

One night a long time ago—but also a long time after that affair on the bridge—Gail woke from a bad dream and urgently confessed something that since then she's never repeated. While the record player was sailing through the air, before it drowned in the river, she heard voices singing: Terrible, chanting voices, overlaying music that sounded like out-of-tune instruments filled with rattling teeth. She said she heard Joey's voice on that record. Never mind that the words were Russian, or that they were muffled through the leather case, or that she was frantic and near screaming...she knew Joey's voice, and she *knew* it was him.

Anyway, once the suitcase went underwater, it was all over. That was Rasputin's weakness—drowning—and it translated to the record player. Gail said I then fell asleep, and I slept for three days straight. She brought me back to her house and nursed me until I woke. After I regained consciousness, she offered to take me home to Les Deux Oies, but I declined. I figured there was nothing of value left there, and I have no idea whatever became of the items in my apartment.

We're married and live in Manhattan now. I've never attended a baggage auction since the last one with Ray, in which I blew twenty bucks just because I had to bid on something. I guess that's a symptom of gambling addiction and a sign to call it quits. Of course I knew I wouldn't attend another auction anyway, because I wouldn't be able to stomach living through the memories, standing before an auctioneer and imagining Joey next to me waving his crippled hand up in the air.

I still watch the pony races from time-to-time, and I still collect, but only one thing, and Gail keeps a tight rein on that. I maintain a collection of postcards from Detroit. Old postcards, nothing newer than 1970, and only those showing scenic locations of the city. Another stipulation of the collection is that the cards must have been postmarked and sent. Unused postcards that never served their purpose—never traveled as they should—just wouldn't do.

I used to visit antique stores, perusing for these old cards, but the first time I saw a gramophone for sale I walked out and haven't set foot in any such place again. It's easier now with the internet, and I can search online for them. I've not returned to Motor City, and all my own photographs are gone, left behind in the apartment, so each old postcard I collect is meaningful.

A new millennium is coming, but the passage of decades does nothing to diminish the pain and sorrow of what occurred that long-ago summer. I suppose that's why I collect old Detroit postcards. Although my last week there was spent in the shadows of a nightmare, the cards harken back to all the other good years. They feature landmarks I was familiar with and often bring rise to fond memories, like the Penobscot Building, Belle Isle Park, and Tiger Stadium. I've got countless cards showing Ambassador Bridge, and I even have one featuring a front view of Les Deux Oies. Imagine my astonishment when I read the script at the bottom of that card's backside, sharing well wishes to his grandchildren: it was signed from George R. Landis...the oldest tenant of the building.

There might even be another reason I collect old postcards. It reminds me of the views of peoples' lives I once stored in trunks and chests, glimpses into their existence. I once collected their trappings and memories in my room, keeping them alive simply by my acknowledgement and my possession. If I'd destroyed those items, it would have been as if they never existed. But I kept them around, and their stories persevered.

And isn't perseverance what immortality is all about?

I'm keeping alive my memories of Detroit through these postcards, and maybe someone will keep alive my memories after I pass.

And that gets me wondering if there might even be *another* reason I collect…was there an underlying motive I kept sent postcards? Why was I compelled to continue to save people's voices? Postcards, like photographs, like albums, are recordings of people's existence. During the time Rasputin had a hold on me, how much of my soul did he carry away? Are there bits and flakes missing, screaming somewhere for me to resurrect them through a few magic words? Does a little part of me still reside in that nightmare land and, when I die, will it return to me, or I to it?

Perhaps saving voices is a means of self-preservation.

Or, perhaps, I'm wasting too much thought worrying about it. I'm an old man without many years left. I won't let time take those while I'm not paying attention to what really matters in life.

Gail's in the next room, and I might just go in there and kiss her with my scarred lip. I might just tell her something that I've said a hundred times before, though I don't think she ever tires of hearing it…

She's the best bid I ever won.

The End

Eric J. Guignard writes and edits dark fiction from his office in Los Angeles. He has over fifty publishing credits for stories and articles in magazines, journals, and anthologies. Although his passion is for fiction, he's also a technical writer and a published essayist including such diverse topics as genealogy, woodworking, banking, and ecology.

Eric is also an anthology editor, including: *Dark Tales of Lost Civilizations* (2012, Dark Moon Books), which was nominated for a Bram Stoker Award®, and this year's critically acclaimed release, *After Death...* (2013, Dark Moon Books).

He's a member of the Horror Writer's Association, the Greater Los Angeles Writer's Society, and is also the Horror Genre Correspondent for *Men's Confidence Magazine*. When not writing, Eric designs and builds custom furniture and is an amateur entomologist.

Most importantly, Eric is married to his high school sweetheart, Jeannette, and father to an adventuresome toddler son, Julian James.

Visit Eric at: www.ericjguignard.com, or at his blog: www.ericjguignard.blogspot.com, or on Twitter: https://twitter.com/ericjguignard.